PENDRAGON

AND THE

SORCERER'S DESPAIR

C.J. BROWN

PENDRAGON LEGEND
BOOK FIVE:

PENDRAGON AND THE SORCERER'S DESPAIR

JOIN C.J. BROWN'S NEWSLETTER

CONTENTS

Newsletter

About the Author

Request for Reviews

Also by C.J. Brown

For my readers--You inspire me.

PROLOGUE

In the dark age of Brittania, three thousand years before Arthur
Land's End

DUST FELL FROM THE CEILING as blocks of stone rained upon the city. An iron sconce fell from the wall to the stone floor and its fire began scorching the oaken doors of the temple.

"My lady, we must go," the Guardian said. From outside, they could hear the clangor of steel and the shouts of men as another round of stone struck the temple.

"My lady, we can't stay."

"There will be nowhere to run if the evil that has awoken lives on," Enya said, watching the great bonfire, contained atop a ring of steps at the center of the temple in a ring of stone. Around it, the warlocks and witches of

1

Demetia stood and watched as the fire shifted, guttered, and began to fade.

"Use anything you can find," Enya said. "This fire must not go out."

Payjen looked at her uncertainly as the rest of the guards eyed the sorcerers who stared at the fire.

"Use everything," he said, angrily. "Oil, benches, anything."

At once, the Guardians started throwing the torches at the fire and breaking the benches to fuel it. One guard carried a pile of old books to the flames, but Payjen stopped him.

"Those are the sacred scrolls," he said. "They cannot burn."

"Those scrolls will mean nothing if this fire goes out, Captain," Enya said. "Those pages are just pages. Burn the books." Payjen didn't say anything, but he looked back at the Guardian, and nodded.

The warrior stepped forward and threw the books at the fire. Red embers flew as another Guardian tossed an oaken leg from one of the chairs.

—

"Your Grace! Your Grace!"

Mergus Megolin turned to see a captain running up to him, his armor dented and spattered with blood. "Your Grace! The enemy have captured the harbor! The people can't escape!"

Mergus turned to see the dock.

Billowing flames sent great columns of smoke toward the heavens as red embers swirled around the sails of the war galleys and merchant ships. Northern mercenaries were battling Demetian soldiers and the water itself was afire as burning driftwood floated around the ships.

Mergus turned to Fergus. "Rally your Highlanders. Go to the oak grove and take out the catapults. Ergar's archers will be there as well. Eliminate both, and that will let our men fight without fire raining from the skies."

"At once, Your Grace."

Fergus turned and galloped off, the hooves of his horse striking the cobblestone road.

He raised his golden greatsword as he thundered by the gate of the Green Keep. "Men of Caledonia!" He yelled. "Warriors of the north!"

Another round of fire raced through the sky.

It struck one of the watchtowers, setting the stones to flying out as the tower began to collapse.

Men shouted as they ran to avoid the stones, and the watchtower fell with a deafening roar.

The hiss of arrows sounded nearby as Demetian archers let fly a flight of arrows that arced through the sky and fell on the battlefield.

"Brothers!" Fergus yelled. "The enemy has already captured the harbor. Most of our men are pinned here! But the fight's not over. Ergar's archers and catapults are firing from the oak grove! We take them out, and we may just get a chance to break free of this trap! Now charge with me!"

The cavalry yelled and thundered after their general, swords drawn.

The northerners battled what remained of the infantry just a few yards away.

Some of them ran aside when they saw the line of Caledonian cavalry charging toward them.

Fergus' horse reared when it reached the enemy ranks and he slashed at one of the soldiers standing near him.

The rest of the cavalry collided with the block of steel. Their horses' iron hooves kicked the northerners where their surcoats were emblazoned with the shining blade of Ergar as the men cut down mercenaries and their fellow Highlanders alike who had remained loyal to the Fallen King.

As Fergus' blade sheared through the mail and tunic of another soldier, another lunged at his courser with his ax.

The sunlight glinted off the blade and caught Fergus' attention. He slashed at the man, cutting his arm off at the elbow. Blood gushed from where his arm had been and he staggered back, screaming.

Fergus cut down another one of the soldiers and looked to see the rest of his cavalry, cutting through the enemy's ranks. But the oak grove was still five hundred yards away, and there were twenty thousand men standing between the Green Keep and the trees that sheltered the catapults and the archers.

—

Mergus' horse whickered and neighed as it stood by the gate of the keep.

The air was heavy with smoke and embers, making breathing itself painful as the air seared his lungs, but that was the least of his concerns right now. To the north, the plaza was burning. The shops and alehouses were wreathed with billowing flames, and there were still soldiers fighting amidst the streets, shrouded with smoke.

To the west, Demetian blood was reddening the waters of the Emerald Sea as the ships burned. As Mergus looked at the harbor, an explosion from one of the ships sent clouds of fire and a wave of splinters flying out. The buckets of tar it had been carrying fell, burning, to the water, and men fighting to get back to shore were engulfed by the flames.

Mergus looked at the men standing with him.

The archers were loosing every arrow they could find, while the rest stood still, watching the battle with eyes cold as ice.

But Mergus could feel their distress. He could hear the thoughts of fear that they screamed, and he could sense their dread, their hollow, withering dread.

He was about to say something when he felt a sharp pain stab through his chest.

He looked and saw the white fletching of the arrow that sheared through his collarplate. Then another arrow struck him, and this time, some of the soldiers heard.

They turned and saw their king with two arrows bristling from his chest.

"No!" one of them said. He raised his shield, and others did the same. His shield stopped another arrow that would have hit their king.

Mergus felt his blood leak out of his armor, and he fell from his horse. His armor clattered when he struck the stone ground.

"Where is my son?" he said. "Where is my son?"

At once, the standard-bearer ran off, looking for the prince as Mergus lay by his horse, watching the sky, black with smoke.

–

One of the warlocks winced as another round of stone struck the temple.

He staggered back and nearly fell, but caught himself with the iron rings that normally held the sconces.

"Toryen," Enya said, frowning.

He looked at her, his yellow eyes growing dark.

"The light is fading," he said. "King Mergus is dying."

Payjen looked at them, confused.

"But…the fire."

"The darkness is growing unstoppable," Enya cut him off, and turned back to Toryen. "Don't distract from the fire," she said. "Do not fall asleep."

–

The sword swept by his eyes, nearly cutting through his

nose, but the man was too far off to reach him. When the blade arced away, Mergyle lunged, cutting the man down.

Around him, Demetian warriors and Royal Guards were maintaining a line of shields, cutting down the enemy by reaching over the iron disks.

Mergyle stepped up to the shields and slashed at a soldier about to cut down one of the Demetian soldiers.

"Watch out!" A voice shouted. He turned to see a spear flying towards him. He moved aside, and the weapon flew past and clattered when it landed.

"Prince Mergyle!" another person shouted. Footsteps hurrying towards him. He turned and saw a man with a pothelm running to him.

"Your father requests your presence! He has been wounded."

Mergyle looked at him, not able to believe what he'd just heard.

The man turned and started running back, and Mergyle followed. His thoughts were centered around his father. All he could think about was the last time they'd seen each other, a day past, before Ergar's army arrived at the city. They had been planning their attack. Mergyle was to attack Ergar's right flank with his cavalry while Mergus attacked the left flank and Fergus attacked the main line. But Mergyle had wanted to attack the main line and argued with his father when he heard his orders. None of what they had planned happened, and now Mergyle refused to believe that he must lose his father when the last time they spoke it had been an argument.

Mergyle followed the man back to the main gate of the keep as another round of fire raced above and hit the castle. A pile of stones fell away, roaring when they crashed.

Some of the lesser stones fell upon the army, but the soldiers raised their shields and they clattered off the iron disks.

Mergyle saw his father just a moment later, lying by his horse.

The archers by the gate were loosing flight after flight of arrows at the enemy as the storm of swords raged just yards away.

Mergyle knelt beside his father. "Father," he said.

Mergus' eyes opened, and he smiled. "Son," he said. "I feared you were lost."

"No, I'm not. And you aren't going to be either."

"Mergyle, we all knew this day was near."

"Father, don't say that."

Mergyle began to sob. He remembered the last thing he had said to his father, and he could feel the guilt and anger poisoning his thoughts.

"Mergyle, this is no time to dwell upon the past. You must care only about the future. What wounds we may have caused each other, they're healed. Focus, my child. And remember, I may be gone after this, but like or ancestors, I will still be here with you. And you must make sure that the light survives. The darkness cannot be allowed to reign. It cannot. The Ergar we are fighting now is the not the man we knew a decade ago. That Ergar is gone. And now we must save what there is left from this monster."

One of the soldiers fell beside them, blood leaking from where a javelin had struck his chest.

The sound of clattering hooves reached his ears, and Mergyle turned to see Fergus galloping towards him.

"Mergyle," his father said, and he turned back to him.

"Do not let your emotions cloud your judgement. Do not let anger and pain steer you wrong. I love you, son."

"Father, I'm so sorry," Mergyle cried. "I love you too."

But his father was not there anymore. His eyes stared blankly. Mergyle's tears washed away the soot that had blackened his face.

He could not hear anything else, and his mind thought of nothing but his father.

"Your Grace!" A voice yelled.

Mergyle turned, still not able to pry himself away from his tears.

"Your Grace! The cavalry has been dispersed. We cannot make it to the catapults," Fergus shouted.

Mergyle looked at him, then looked beyond at the battlefield.

He stood.

"I don't care," he growled. "Call every close-combat

soldier we have. The archers will remain and guard the keep. The rest of us are shattering the northerners."

Fergus looked at him.

He nodded and galloped off.

Mergyle turned, a black storm upon his face, his cloak swirling amidst the toxic air.

He walked past the line of archers, and they looked at him with shock.

"Your Grace!" They started yelling.

But Mergyle did not answer.

A thunderous roar sounded from the right and Mergyle turned to see Demetians and Fergus' northerners fight their way through the block of soldiers, rallying soldiers from the field of single combat to their side.

"Archers!" Mergyle yelled. "Keep loosing! I want the sky alight with fire arrows."

"Yes, Your Grace!" The archers said.

They set their arrows afire and loosed.

As a flight of a thousand arrows, trailing fire and smoke, raced through the sky, Mergyle turned and walked towards the site of the battle just yards away beyond the spiked trenches and moats.

Just a few feet from the moat, he started running.

The steel armor and weapons of the enemy reflected the wave of fire arrows that arced through the air and began to fall.

Launching when he reached the moat, he soared through the air, poised to strike, as he fell toward the ranks of fighting soldiers. He landed, cutting down the first northerner, as the arrows fell on the soldiers.

Some of their own men were hit, but most were able to escape the arrows for them to find the surcoats of their enemies. Shrill shouts and screams sounded from the battlefield as soldiers, with their backs engulfed by flame, ran, looking to douse the fire. Mergyle slashed at one of the Ergar soldiers and then lunged at another.

The man's kite shield stopped his blade, but Mergyle just attacked again, and cut off the man's legs.

Leaving him to his agony, he cut down another soldier and looked to see Fergus battling his way towards him.

Another flight of fire arrows fell upon the battlefield, as a line of burning tar catapulted from the oak grove. They raced toward the Keep, trailing smoke. Chunks of the castle broke away. Fires erupted throughout the yard, and guards ran from the battlements as they fell away.

—

"The fire, it's stable now," Payjen said, stepping back as one of the guards tossed another book at the bonfire.

And then a great roar sounded. The crash of stone could be heard from outside, and dust fell from the ceilings as a line sprouted across the north wall and the ceiling.

"Payjen, there is no way out of here," Enya said. "The Keep is surrounded by the enemy. But we will fight till the very end." Payjen and the Guardians looked at her. "Aye," Payjen said. "To the end."

A solemn silence fell on the temple. The fires of the

battle could be seen through the windows and the clangor of steel and the shouts of agony could be heard.

"They are with us," Enya said, "all of our brothers and sisters who fell to The Cleansing. They are here now. And we are about to see them."

Payjen turned at the sound of steel crashing through a door and men shouting as their steps echoed through the hall.

"Soldiers!" He yelled as he drew his sword.

The Guardians drew their weapons and formed two ranks before the bonfire.

–

Mergyle cut down another northerner, fighting beside Fergus and his soldiers before the gates of the Keep. An arrow raced past his head, and Mergyle turned to see an archer standing amidst the soldiers, notching another arrow.

He ran towards him, and before the soldier could draw, he slashed, cutting through his surcoat, hauberk, and tunic.

The man fell forward and Mergyle was about to slash at another soldier when they heard a loud roar like metal screeching and turned to see the keep.

Ergar's army was concentrating at the western Sea Gate. A great stone seemed to have wrenched the portcullis and the enemy was pouring through.

Mergyle turned to Fergus.

"Double back to the keep! They're getting through."

He turned and ran back, cutting down Ergar soldiers as they ran for the gate.

Fergus yelled at his men to turn back, and soon, the army of two thousand northerners were fighting their way back to the Keep.

Mergyle cut down another one of Ergar's soldiers and turned to Fergus. "We've got to cut them off!"

Fergus looked at the column of soldiers pouring through the gate.

He turned to his men. "Form a line and charge!" He yelled. "We'll surround them!"

They turned and hurried off, and the soldiers forwarded his orders as Mergyle and Fergus reached the river of soldiers storming the gate.

Mergyle cut down one as Fergus slashed at another.

He looked to see the two thousand friendly northerners trying to shatter the river of enemies.

He turned back to the soldiers before him and cut them down.

–

The soldiers collided with the barred doors as Payjen and his men stood by the bonfire, watching the oak panels.

The enemy shouted as they struck the doors again.

"Soldiers, we are the Guardians of Light, we are the protectors of the Temple." They all began chanting their words. "We oppose all evil. We uphold the good. For eternity, our lives guard the House of Light! Bright are our minds and stone is our will! We fear no danger, fear no threat but the darkness. We are the Guardians of the Temple!" The oak bar splintered and snapped, and the doors flew open.

The torrent of steel poured through, racing toward the bonfire.

Payjen and his men met enemy blades with their own, and the Temple resounded with the clash of steel. As the fighting went on just yards away, Enya stared at the fire.

She began to chant, and the other witches and warlocks followed suit. Their voices carried their words beyond the battle, beyond the roof of the Temple, and to the heavens. As they chanted, Enya looked to see northerners falling before the line of guardians, and then the first of them fell.

The warrior collapsed before the bonfire, and then another fell when a spear sprouted from his shoulder.

Payjen slashed at a northern soldier when an arrow cut through his collarplate, and he staggered back.

The chant continued, and light began to shine from their eyes.

Payjen stabilized himself before attacking another. He met the soldier's uppercut, pushed his blade away, and lunged at the man, shearing through his surcoat and mail.

Around him, the Guardians were falling, and the fire was already guttering out.

Payjen slashed at another northerner, and then he buckled when a greatsword sprouted from his side.

Enya saw him spit blood, and then slash the man who had stabbed him.

The greatsword withdrew, and his blood spilled on the steps to the bonfire. Another Guardian fell beside him, and the northerners ran past their line, towards the witches and warlocks, shouting.

One of them raised their blade to strike Toryen, but when the greatsword fell, it cut through air, and Toryen remained standing.

"The light will always shine!" Payjen yelled, rising. An arrow found his back, and he nearly fell, but he kept himself up.

Around him, the last of the Guardians, five wounded men, rose from the stone ground, red with the blood of their brethren.

The northerner who'd tried to kill Toryen turned to see Payjen, arrows bristling from his shoulder and back, standing.

He turned and charged back at him.

Payjen darted aside when the Highlander raised his sword and slashed at him.

He turned and cut off the arm of another, and was about to slash a third, when the cold steel of his enemy's blade drove through his chest.

Enya felt anger, grief, and regret welling, regret that they could not have helped them. They had tried, but whatever they had done clearly wasn't enough. She felt grief as friends and family who had been by their side for decades fell, and anger as she saw the last of the light beginning to go out.

Her thoughts switched to Mergyle. The new king was cutting through the column of soldiers storming the gate with Fergus and his northerners. With red eyes and a black storm upon his face, grief and anger propelled him. He was not of the darkness, but there was no light either. Enya's sight returned to the temple, and she could see the guardians lying upon the ground, their weapons at their side.

Payjen was lying by the steps, his green eyes blank, blood still pouring from his wounds.

The northerners ran through Toryen and the other warlocks.

"Find them!" One of them yelled. "They couldn't have gone far!"

Toryen looked at Enya. "So, we're gone then."

Enya looked at all of them. "Until such time as the light can truly return to the Isle, our souls will remain here, neither dead nor living. The centuries will go past. We will see cities rise and fall. We will see the end of this war, the generations that go by, and we will see whether our people emerge from the darkness."

—

Fergus and Mergyle ran through the gate, slashing at northern soldiers as their own men poured through. The yard was crowded with soldiers as the enemy stormed the battlements and tried to get through the doors to the Temple and the rest of the Keep. Mergyle drove his blade through the surcoat of one soldier, slashed at another, and

16

caught an arrow as it raced toward him. An Ergar soldier, shouting as he ran, ran toward him, his ax held high.

Mergyle let the soldier charge at him, and just as he was about to strike, Mergyle lunged and cut off his arms.

The man didn't even yell.

Mergyle turned and saw the soldiers rushing through the doors and running to the Temple. He ran after them, cutting down enemy soldiers when they tried to attack him as soldiers battled around him. He reached the snapped and splintered oak doors and slashed at one Ergar soldier.

The Demetian warriors spotted their king and ran to him as Mergyle slashed and cut his way through.

There was only one line of soldiers running past, so Mergyle did not find himself terribly outnumbered. And then his men arrived, and they cut down the enemy with almost no fight.

Mergyle ran straight for the Temple doors, cutting down an enemy soldier only when one tried to slay him.

That's when he saw the Guardians.

Soldiers shouted around him, and the stone hall echoed the clangor of steel as the torches cast a shadow of the battle upon the bricks, and Mergyle's heart turned heavy.

He could see the fallen Guardians before the bonfire, and none of the warlocks were there.

—

THIRTY YEARS BEFORE THE HUNS ATTACK
IN THE WIZARD'S PLANE

Stars shone amidst the night sky. As white points of light, they kept the worst of the darkness at bay. Enya looked at them, watching as the trees rustled and the great fires at the top of the watchtowers guttered. She looked towards the oak grove. The streets between the trees and the Green Keep had once been the site of fire, pain, and battle. She remembered the houses that had burned, the stone buildings that had collapsed from the fires, the clash of steel and the shouting. She remembered the day Land's End fell, the time madness stepped out of the shadows, the time all human character failed.

"My lady," Toryen said. "You seem disturbed."

Enya looked at him. "It's nothing. I just still remember that day."

"We all do," Toryen said. "But we can find a way to make things right."

"I know. Any premonitions?"

"Not as of yet," Toryen said. "For that, I'm grateful."

"Good," Enya said. "How are the others?"

"Solemn as always." His yellow eyes scanned the horizon, as if looking for some threat.

"I can still remember the smoke," he said. "You could see it from ten miles away."

"Best not dwell," Enya said, but she knew it was easier to say than to actually move on. That day had been the worst of Britannian history. And not because a city had been burned, but because the lives who were lost that day, were lost at the hands of those whom they believed to be friends. All the world had believed Ergar to be the one who would end the centuries of civil war amongst the peoples of the Isle. And for ten years, he was the friend and king Britons had been looking for. But what the warlocks could not see was that there was darkness hidden amidst the light of the Chosen King, darkness that had not been tampered or dealt with. Darkness alone did not drive Ergar mad. It was his lacking will that let the darkness consume him, poison his mind, and poison his world. The idea that he was a chosen one made him arrogant, made him paranoid, afraid that another might wish to overthrow him. Mergus tried to convince him of the truth, but Ergar would not see it. He called Mergus a traitor and accused him of plotting to steal the throne. And then he sent Lord Fergus to attack Demetia, but neither he nor his soldiers were willing to carry out the orders of a mad king, and to attack brothers. So, Ergar cast him out as well, and raised a mercenary army of a hundred thousand to quell all those who opposed him.

There were warlocks everywhere at the time, and the world knew that warlocks all derived their power from Demetia. Ergar feared they worked for Mergus, and so he executed them. And just a year after the war had begun, the Isle had changed forever. Most of the warlocks were gone. All those who remained were at Land's End and Demetia. Entire cities had been torched. Entire fields had been turned to muddy wastelands, and Ergar's madness grew beyond hope. A dark shadow fell upon the lands he controlled. Fearful of opposition, the cities that had survived the fire were controlled by mercenaries. The blade replaced the law, and a criminal was a criminal if judged so by Ergar. People managed to escape, crossing the border to Demetia, Land's End, and the last of the free realms. As the war continued, Mergus and his armies fought to keep the northern storm back. But no matter the battles when they defeated Ergar, Mergus knew the light was fading. Darkness truly displaced all the light when the last of their allies defected to Ergar's side, and all who remained were the northern soldiers commanded by Fergus, and Demetia. Three years after the war began, Ergar's armies reached the capital of Land's End. Demetia had already fallen, and its survivors staged a last stand at the fishing town. The warlocks and witches perished that day, and all light had gone out. But Mergus' heir, Mergyle, was able to send the northern armies retreating, though at great cost. When word of this turn of events reached their former allies, they rejoined their banners, and marched to Pittentrail, freeing cities as they went.

Months later, they arrived at the capital of Caledonia. Ergar, not able to comprehend what had happened, fled. No one ever saw him again. Excalibur, the great sword of kings that Ergar had wielded, could only be wielded by he who was worthy, and had now been left behind. Warlocks could carry it too, though they could not wield it. If they tried to cut someone down, the blade would stop before it reached their target.

Mergyle melted the blade and forged sixteen new ones from it. None of them contained the magic of the one blade, so others could wield them. The blades were given to the sixteen kings of the Isle, for them to safeguard and wait for a time when another, wiser and truer than Ergar, appeared.

No one had, and the three-thousand-year-old prophecy faded away to legend.

But the warlocks remembered. Enya removed herself from her thoughts and returned her focus to the present world. She remembered the fields were no longer afire, that the city was peaceful, and that things were better than they had ever been. But something still wasn't right. Not all the light had returned, and the warlocks and witches of the Isle were still waiting to return to the land of the living.

Enya turned to see two warlocks walking just outside the main gate, their forms glowing.

She heard the sound of the waves just then, and then she was not standing before the merlons of the keep's bailey, but standing upon the shores of Demetia, looking at the Narrow Sea.

She looked around.

A cold air, frigid and dreary, raced across the beach.

Birds flew out of the trees, squawking and cawing, and that's when she saw it.

A fleet of warships, their sails black with a golden crest. Ranks of galleys and cogs and triremes charged for the shore. Fur-clad men bristled upon the decks, their warhammers and blades reflecting the rings of torches that crackled along the rails.

And then the first galleys were landing, and Enya was watching with fear and dread as the dark warriors, growling and foul, jumped from the ships and ran towards the trees.

One of them was running towards her, and Enya saw that his face was Toryen's, and he was shouting.

Enya awoke to find herself weak and cold.

Toryen was standing beside her, shouting, and the other witches and warlocks were there as well.

"What happened?" Toryen said. "Your eyes turned black."

Enya looked at him. "Darkness," she said.

"What are you talking about?" Another one of the warlocks asked as a Green Keep guard walked through another warlock, not aware at all that ancient spirits stood by him. "I saw a fleet of hundreds of ships. There were thousands of soldiers, all flying the banner of the Huns."

"The Huns?"

"But Emperor Constantine is fighting them now," Toryen said. "They are weak. They could not possibly be planning to attack the Isle."

"This isn't now," Enya told them. "This is decades from now, when the Huns will be commanded by the foulest person who has ever walked."

Toryen thought for a moment.

"What do you suggest we do?" Toryen asked. "We

cannot change the course of events. We can only direct time."

"So that's what we do. For three thousand years, the Isle has not seen more than a few wizards. De Grance's daughter will be born tonight, but Leo fears that neither she nor his wife will see the dawn. I can hear him. He is praying now. Someone must answer."

Toryen looked at her.

"I will," a younger witch said. Enya turned to see her. Her yellow eyes glowed as she looked at her. Her face was kind and her energy, good.

"You know what you will be giving up, Katyana" Enya said. "Once all good returns, all of us will return to the world as we are, and you may know nothing of your true self."

"Why does this have to happen?" Toryen asked. "Why does Lord De Grance's daughter mean anything?"

"The wizard who returns to the world of the living by her is destined to change the course of the future. What I saw, Toryen, will happen. And a second darkness from which we cannot escape will shroud the Isle if we do not act. De Grance is praying for his daughter to live. It is the only chance we have."

"I can do it," the young witch repeated. "I had no family of my own three thousand years ago. I shall have one now. You are my family as well, but I sense we will all perish if this does not happen."

23

Enya looked at her. She knew what Katyana was sacrificing, what she was giving up.

"No," she said. "I'll go."

"Enya, you cannot do this," Toryen argued.

"I'm sorry, Toryen. But this has to be done." She looked back at Katyana.

"I will not let you give up your life. Twenty years from now, when the fight is here, you will fight from this world, and when the light prevails, you will return to the land of the living."

Katyana looked at her. "I have decided," she said. "I will go. I will not die. And maybe one day, I will remember all of this. Now, I must go."

"Katyana," Toryen was saying, but she disappeared.

"She cannot be stopped now," Enya said. "We can only hope that her sacrifice will not be for nothing."

Katyana found herself racing through the night.

Guards walked the streets as chatter drifted out of the taverns and water crashed upon the rocks at the harbor.

But Katyana did not pay that any mind. She was racing for the top of the Green Keep.

Flying past guards and mortared stone, she reached the chamber just moments later.

She could hear the midwife's voice, but not Genie's nor a baby's.

By the rail of the balcony, she walked around to find De Grance looking up at the night.

His hands were clasped, and tears were rolling from his eyes.

"Just save my family," he said. "Just save them."

She walked to the doors and looked at the baby. She was swaddled up and silent. The midwife tried to warm her by the fire, but she wouldn't wake. Leo turned and walked past her, straight to his daughter. "There's no heartbeat," the midwife said.

Katyana knew there was no time to reconsider or think. If she did not give life to that baby, she knew dark things were going to happen.

She closed her eyes and chanted a spell.

She felt her memories fade away. She forgot what Enya and the other warlocks taught her. She forgot all she had ever known, and then she remembered nothing. Not even how to speak.

C.J. BROWN

1

HUNTED

In the time of Arthur
In the Enchanted Forest

ORSES NEIGHED AND REARED, kicking up dirt with their hooves as they thundered away from the city. The Huns shrieked behind them as Demetia and the enchanted forest blazed and burned, sending columns of smoke billowing up. Red embers swirled amidst the trees as the ancient barks collapsed.

The barbarians loosed arrows and hurled spears at the Demetians, killing those at the end of the retreating force.

Merlin raced ahead beside his father, Arthur's body slumped before him as fireballs crashed around them, lighting up the fields.

The sounds of battle could still be heard as Magi Ro

Hul fought the Hun force at the western sectors of the city, distracting them from the retreat. The fierce fighting could be heard and seen from where Megolin was leading the retreat.

Men shouted and fell amidst the melee and the fire.

But Merlin almost couldn't hear it.

He was staring at Arthur, the rest of the world a blurry, chaotic, senseless haze.

This was not supposed to happen. Arthur was the chosen one, predicted by the ancient warlocks to be the one who would unite the lands and bring peace to the Isle. And yet he was dead.

A fireball crashed beside them, scattering burning tar on the ground. The autumn greenery caught the flames and began to burn.

Merlin knew he had to revive Arthur. But he could not do it now, not here. But Arthur's soul would be lost forever beyond hope of returning to this world if it was not kept here.

Merlin closed his eyes and chanted an ancient chant. Slurring syllables and words of an ancient language made it past the din of battle.

Ascending to the stars, they seemed to sound in every corner of the world, till Merlin opened his eyes and saw Arthur's skin glowing blue. His spirit would be contained. Merlin would be able to reach his soul him to revive him.

"Stay together!" Megolin shouted as the Highlander horses carried the civilians and the wounded away.

A Hun arrow found the side of one of the Demetian cavalry and the man fell over.

His horse thundered away, leaving him behind.

Spears and arrows and stones crisscrossed the air. Fire crashed down around them as twenty thousand Huns with their banners caught high by the wind chased them.

As the sun rose higher, Demetia burned. Huns looted the sacred temple and the great hall, where Arthur had first met King Megolin. The palace was looted, and the streets littered with the fallen and the ruins of the buildings. The oak structures were burning uncontrollably, collapsing from the fire, and could be heard from a mile away.

Merlin turned back and witnessed the carnage that the Huns dealt.

Ten thousand had been running from Demetia, and two thousand of them had fallen defending the retreat.

At once, the wind began to swirl. The fires were pushed back, and the great currents sent dust and dirt flying up.

Cloaks snapped in the whirlwind as Merlin focused it around the barbarians attacking them. The fury of the winds mustered as much sand and dirt from the plains of Demetia as a minor sandstorm of Arabia. Hurting the eyes of the barbarians and setting them to coughing, the wind broke their attack, leaving the rest of the column to charge away from the battle.

The storm began to dissipate, and Merlin turned back, staring west.

An hour later, they were two leagues from the city, and had lost the Huns.

The hooves of Merlin's horse struck the muddy ground of the rutted road as it strode west. Megolin sat silently beside him, and Igraine to his right. From the rest of the column, they could hear the rattle of wagons and the groaning of the wounded.

Arthur's body still glowed blue, and Merlin could sense his presence.

He closed his eye and tried to reach him.

A gust of wind sent the golden leaves that were piled across the road whirling around them. The thistles and hedges that lined it bristled, and the sky began to darken.

Megolin looked up and saw the clouds gathering. A bolt of lightning lit up the world, and the thunder roared.

Megolin looked at Merlin.

His eyes were glowing white.

Merlin found himself standing amidst a dark world, lit by a thousand and more stars.

When he looked down, there was no ground, only more of those shining lights.

The realm of the elders was a solemn place, and yet Merlin felt peaceful here. He did not feel the fatigue of war, or the fear that battle caused. He felt strong.

"Arthur!" he said.

Arthur appeared before him, but without his wounds. His form, Roman armor, and cloak, glowed white. He did not seem to have any of the wounds he'd been dealt. The arrows that had killed him were gone, and he was smiling.

"Arthur. I'm here to bring you back," Merlin said.

Arthur seemed not to notice.

"Have you seen this place before?" Arthur asked.

"No."

"It is peaceful. There is no war, no corrupt souls fighting for power. Just peace, and truth, and those we thought we lost forever. I have spoken with my father, you know, and Olivie."

Merlin looked at him sadly. Arthur's look appeared to be one of peace, but for a man who had endured so much pain, Merlin knew it was a look of hopelessness.

"Arthur," Merlin told him. "The world is growing dark."

Arthur looked at him, and his smile faded.

"Demetia has fallen. The Huns are overrunning everything. Mehmet attacks from the north. Thousands have died, and the future of the Isle, of all peoples, is at stake."

"I am done with that world," Arthur said, venomously, scowling. "That world has offered me nothing but grief and pain, nothing but war and suffering. I am done with it."

Merlin stepped back.

"But Arthur, you were the one the warlocks predicted would unite the Isle. You are the one who would wield

Excalibur. You are the one would bring peace. If you do not return, all is lost."

Arthur looked at him angrily. "All is lost," he said. "My death proves it. Perhaps you'll be here as well soon. You will be peaceful here, I promise you."

Arthur began to disappear.

"Arthur!" Merlin shouted, but Arthur was gone. But Arthur had never been there, Merlin realized. It was a broken man Merlin had spoken to, not the general he had met a lifetime ago.

Still, Merlin could not leave Arthur there. He needed to return.

He must, or all would fall to darkness, and his soul with it.

He began to draw Arthur's spirit back to his body.

The wind howled around them, and the horses neighed and whickered, afraid.

The Demetian soldiers were accustomed to the magic of their lords, but the Highlanders were less certain, and looked about with doubt and fear, scanning the trees.

Megolin noticed that the blue containment that anchored Arthur's spirit was glowing brighter.

But Merlin's face was of anguish.

Then a wave of energy raced from him, snapping branches and sending the leaves rustling back. Megolin nearly fell off his horse as the rest around them reared and neighed.

Igraine managed to keep from falling, and Arthur's body almost hadn't moved.

The clouds began to clear, and light returned to the road.

Merlin fell off his horse and landed beside Megolin's destrier, his cloak splattered with mud.

"Son," Megolin said, swinging down from his saddle.

"I failed," Merlin said. "I failed. Arthur is broken. He does not want to return, and I didn't have the power to revive him."

Igraine looked at him. His yellow eyes were dim.

"Arthur is still there, Merlin. You must not despair," she said, hiding the pain she felt. Her husband was gone, lost forever, when he had just returned to her, and now she was at the doorstep of losing her son as well.

Megolin helped Merlin back up.

They strode on, and the column resumed its march.

"You two," Merlin heard Clyde order his soldiers, "double-back and scout the way we marched. Make sure no one is following us. And do not attack if you see the Huns."

"Aye, my lord," one of them said, and the two soldiers wheeled their horses around and galloped off beside the column.

As the sound of their hooves striking the dirt road faded away, Merlin searched his soul for answers.

His friend was broken. He knew that, and yet he could

not understand it. He had never endured such peril nor such pain. All his family had, and he had been spared.

How do I heal him when I do not know his pain?

"We'll stop here," Megolin announced at mid-day, after the scouts returned to report that no one was following. "Water your horses, and rest. We'll be moving again soon."

Merlin reined his horse as the column halted.

General Clyde posted soldiers around them a quarter of a league away, each with a horn to warn if the enemy was seen.

Merlin turned to Verovingian.

"Find an empty wagon," he told him, his voice tired. "Arthur and his father must rest as well."

Verovingian nodded sadly and turned to find an empty wagon.

He wouldn't, he supposed, but he would just move the stuff a full one carried.

Merlin swung down from his horse along with Megolin and Igraine. The soldiers were walking off the road to sit by the trees and drink and wash their faces of dirt and blood and grief. There were no streams nearby, and Megolin was not going to let any of his people wander far. As it was, eight thousand souls, soldiers, children, women, the old, and the sick, marching as one, was dangerous. With an army of almost a hundred thousand just a few leagues back, they were an obvious target. It was not safe for any of them to break from the column.

Merlin turned at the sound of a cart rattling and Verovingian's horse plodding towards him.

Merlin heaved Arthur's armored body, bristling with arrows, off his horse and walked to the cart.

Megolin followed with Uther, and they placed them on the wood.

Uther's eyes were closed, and the arrow that hit him was still there.

"I will remove them," Igraine said. "As my husband's wife and my son's mother."

Merlin nodded and walked away with Megolin.

Igraine turned to her family.

She felt tears welling and almost felt like she might faint, but she remained still as stone. She could not weep. She could not be weak.

She reached and removed the arrow from her husband's bronze armor.

The arrow scratched the breach it had made as it withdrew from Uther.

She cast the arrow down and held her husband's hand.

She did not notice it, but the entire column was watching her. Some of them cried. Others finally turned away, and the rest watched, silent, paying their respects. Her people were foreigners, but Igraine was one of them. Regardless, a fallen soul was a fallen soul, wherever it was from. And Gaea recognized all, whether they believed it was real or not.

"Rest, my love," she told her husband. "I'm glad we found our peace before the end."

She removed the arrows from her son.

"Arthur," she told him, "if you can hear me, you are not broken. You are a Pendragon, and to be a Pendragon is to rise above our demons. Your grandfather was a flawed man, and your father better. You shall rise as well. Do not let despair and pain steal the future that is your destiny and the destiny of all those living and not yet living of this land."

She covered them with the woolen cloth at the side of the wagon.

Merlin turned away and walked off to one of the oak trees.

He sat beside it and leaned on the gnarled bark.

The green smell of fields and forests were far more refreshing than the fumes of fire and battle.

Merlin retrieved his waterskin and drank from the leather pouch. But the water was not cool, or comforting. It was scalding, and the taste was rancid.

It tastes of war, he thought.

But how could the water from his skin be so toxic? The streams that ran near Demetia were clear and clean and fresh, not sickening.

"The water is bad," he heard his father say.

He looked up from the waterskin to look at Megolin.

"I do not know why."

Megolin sat beside him.

"Your grandfather used to say the water was rank whenever he failed at something. It always tasted as clean to me. Perhaps not being a warlock has spared me from such things. It also has limited me as well. But you are not limited, my son. You are powerful, but you lack confidence. I may be no warlock, but I understand that the universe and time itself always tends to good. Trust that, and you will not be disappointed."

Merlin considered what his father said, and nodded, setting the skin aside.

Merlin was about to say something when a low rumble roared through the trees. Birds rushed up, startled, and the horses neighed.

Megolin bolted up, and Merlin stood as well.

All eyes were looking north, where one of the sentries had been posted. Then the horn sounded again.

"Get moving!" Megolin bellowed, running to his horse as soldiers and civilians reformed the column.

He vaulted up, then Merlin did the same. Igraine was there, and General Clyde.

"Charge!" Megolin yelled. "Now!"

They spurred their horses forward and galloped off, followed by eight thousand souls ahorse and afoot.

The Megolin banner flew above them as the horses thundered away and the rest ran as speedily as they could.

Shouts of panic could be heard from the column, and babies were crying from the horn.

The four scouts emerged from the trees ten minutes later and charged beside them.

Megolin gave no mind to them and turned to see his people.

They were bristling, pushing past each other, running as fast as they could go. A wagon carrying a dozen people rattled at the side of the road, lurching as it rolled over stones and hedges.

Soldiers were trying to calm the people with shouts, but their words were drowned by fear.

Merlin turned to see the wagon bearing Arthur and Uther rattling away, its wheels spinning and kicking up dirt as the draft horse galloped.

An hour later, Megolin sent one of the scouts to check if they were still being followed.

The man appeared beside Megolin and shook his head.

Merlin's father reared his horse.

Merlin, Igraine, and Clyde did the same, and the people almost tripped as they stopped.

"They'll find us again," Megolin said. "We should get off the road. And light no fires."

"You heard His Grace!" General Clyde yelled when no one moved. "Clear the road!"

At once, horses and people began melting away behind the trees at the right of the road. Drivers led their wagons and carts off the road, making sure their wheels didn't snap upon a rock, or get trapped by mud.

Merlin stayed beside his father, Clyde, Igraine, and the

wagon carrying Arthur and Uther as they watched their people disappear amidst the pines.

Megolin turned his horse toward the trees and strode towards them, followed by his clan.

The ground amidst the thinning trees was a dense layer of autumn leaves.

The air smelled of bark and green. A few green things still grew here and there, but as the world grew colder, growing things seemed to slink away, to leave the world gray and brown.

But at least the trees would hide their numbers. And if Megolin placed his soldiers correctly, any casual eye might mistake them all for warriors. That was unlikely, though it would be better than advertising that they were a miserable band of refugees, most of whom couldn't lift a sword.

"We keep moving," Megolin told his people amidst the gloom of the trees. Shadows cast by the branches lined the fallen leaves. "Get some distance between us and the Huns. We camp at nightfall. But no fires. And I'll want guards watching all directions."

"It will be done, Your Grace," General Clyde said.

Megolin nodded and spurred his horse forward.

Merlin, Igraine, and the driver pulling their kin lurched ahead.

Merlin's hooves jabbed at the carpet of leaves. He could hear them crunching at every step, and the footfalls of the eight thousand were almost too loud for him to bear.

He raised his hood and sat silently.

That night, the rains poured, and the winds shrieked, their gales threatening to tear the pines out, root and all.

Merlin's tent snapped and threatened to fly away.

Merlin was lying on the pile of leaves, his hood up and cloak wrapped around him.

He found himself shivering, his cloak damp from the drops that made it through the tent flaps.

His breath misted before him, and he was trying to sleep.

The rest of the camp was too. Their tents did little to keep the wind and rain out, and Merlin's head rang with the clapping of thunder and the rain falling on the tent like arrows pelting a warrior's helm.

Merlin had already dozed off a few times, but each time he jumped up, panicking. Each time he told himself it was just a dream, yet when he fell asleep again, the nightmare would return.

He saw Arthur, with his Roman cape flowing from his shoulders, his sword resting at his side, bloody.

The point of the blade was resting on a piece of slate, and he almost wasn't holding the hilt.

That was when Merlin would notice the bodies at his feet, and the fires that burned around him, and the arrow that had found his shoulder when he was escaping from Pittentrail with Olivie.

Merlin jumped out of sleep again, his brow dotted with sweat. He turned and craned his neck to look outside the tent. Even hidden beneath the tarp, Merlin could see the glow of Arthur's spirit.

C.J. BROWN

2

DARKNESS CLOSING IN

MORNING ARRIVED WITH A LEAD sky that blocked out most of the sun, leaving the woods damp and flooded from the heavy rains. The ground was a mushy plain of wet leaves and soggy mud that made men have to pull their legs up as they walked.

The downpour had also left many of their people and soldiers blue and sick with cold. And despite their best efforts, all the wagons carrying their limited provisions had been flooded. But it was still edible, so Merlin forced himself to down soggy bread.

But at this point, it didn't matter if it was roast capon. Merlin wouldn't have been able to eat that either. Silence and solemnity hung over the royal table as Megolin, Merlin, and Igraine broke their fast.

As Merlin chewed another chunk of water-soaked bread he could hear the sound of water dripping right outside the tent. With no sun, and with a thicket of trees to shield them from most of the light, nothing had dried. Pools of water had even collected atop some of the larger pavilions and drained with steady drips.

Merlin pitied the two guards who stood outside in the damp and cold. At least here there was a fire crackling, and candles burning all around, emitting a kind of ruddy warmth.

The little fires and the great hearth reflected off the metalwork of their garb and shed light on their forms.

Merlin's purple cloak was glowing red, and his long black hair hung damp and heavy. Dark bags hung beneath his eyes, and his face seemed pale and cold.

Not very different was his father. King Megolin's regal purple cloak was splattered with mud, and his skin looked clammy.

Igraine's eyes were red. Megolin had seen that when they first met for breakfast and had known better than to ask why she had been weeping.

She still wore the armor she had been wearing the day the Huns descended on her home. Most of the blood had been washed off, but there were still signs of battle, dents and scratches and whatnot, that could still be seen.

"Once the people are ready, we resume the march,"

Megolin said suddenly, as he crunched the last slice of bacon, and then used his soggy bread to mop up the oil. Fires were allowed when the sun was out.

"At this rate, we'll arrive at Gilidor within three days."

"The Huns are still pursuing us, brother, I'm sure. And we do not have the strength to fight another battle. Less than half of the people with us are soldiers, and those soldiers we have are either wounded or sick."

"Not all of them," Megolin responded, chewing. "As Commander Clyde tells me, we still have about three hundred capable fighting men."

"If fifty thousand could not defeat them, what makes you think three hundred will?" Merlin said.

Megolin looked at his son.

"We are not looking to fight, Merlin. Right now, our focus is getting to Land's End alive."

"Then we'll have to hasten the march."

"And how do we do that?" Megolin demanded. "Have you seen them? Many are wounded and can only manage a slow walk. Some don't even have legs. Others are dying. The Huns could be on the horizon now, and we wouldn't be going any faster. The best hope we have to is to place as many of our soldiers as we can behind us to guard the column."

Merlin looked back at his own plate. The bacon grease was cooling, and the oil was beginning to congeal. "Yes, Father," he said.

Megolin turned to Igraine.

"I see no better option," she admitted.

"It's settled, then. Page!"

They heard scurrying footsteps, and then the tent flap flew open and a young lad with dark black curls and a mockery of a mustache rushed in, tracking mud on the carpets. But that was the least of Megolin's concerns.

"Your Grace," he said.

"Send for Commander Clyde and the baggage master" Megolin ordered. "Tell them to see me immediately."

"At once, Your Grace."

He bowed and ran out of the pavilion.

A few minutes later, the puffing and the chink of mail signaled Commander Clyde's and the baggage master's arrival. The Megolins rose to greet them as they and Harry, their page, walked through the flap.

Commander Clyde and the baggage master bowed. "Your Grace."

The general wore a black leather jerkin and leather vambraces. Chainmail covered the rest of his arms, and iron poleyns his knees, in addition to the brown breeches he wore.

Without his helm, his poofy patch of white hair stood up from his head unhindered. His skin was marked with the wrinkles and lines of his age, and bags drooped from his lower eyelids. But his cold blue eyes had lost none of their clarity, and they saw with an iron sharpness.

Baggage master Royce was a very different matter, with countless folds that tugged at the buttons of his doublet. His wispy white hair was combed back, and his face was sullen and pasty. He'd never been fair to look upon, but he'd always been a true and loyal friend of the House of Megolin. There were not many people whom Megolin trusted as much as him.

"Gather all the fighting men we have," Megolin said to Clyde. "Send them to the back of the column. Place the wounded at the front and the women and children just behind. And I want scouts keeping a lookout at all times. We march once this is done. And Royce, I want all our provisions locked up and hidden away."

Royce frowned.

"Your Grace?" he asked, surprised.

"Father, the people are starving--"

"And that is the very reason for this," Megolin said sternly. "The road ahead holds desperation for us until we can get to Gilidor. If people start stealing food, fights are going to break out, and the camp will be divided. And that's the last thing we need right now."

He turned back to Royce, a dark storm upon his face. "How much food do we have?"

"Not enough, Your Grace. We only have enough to feed about a third of our column for another day. The retreat was so sudden, and all that we have here is what our people fled away with."

Megolin clenched his fists.

"Ration the food. Divide it however you must. I want everyone fed for at least the next three days. Send word to the high huntsman. He is to find whatever he can within a mile of the column every morning and evening. But he is not to wander off any farther."

"Very good, Your Grace," Royce said, and turned to leave.

Megolin was turning away too when he realized the general was still standing there.

"What is it?" he asked.

Clyde clenched his jaw. "We've already started losing people," he said, quietly.

Megolin straightened.

"How many?"

"Two. Both soldiers. One had a nasty ax wound. Bloody Hun almost cut off his arm at the shoulder. They tried patching him up, but he bled too much, and by last night he was infected. The nurses tell me the wound festered. He died in his sleep. The other lad suffered a club to the head. They said when he woke up, he couldn't remember anything. He died last night."

Merlin looked down at the dirt. This pavilion had been built last night, so the ground here wasn't nearly as soaked as the ground outside.

Megolin shook his head. "These men died from their wounds," he said. "Will we lose anyone else between now and the time we get to Gilidor?"

"I hope we don't, Your Grace," Clyde answered solemnly.

"Have the men dig two graves for them," Megolin ordered. "Are their families with them?"

"Yes, Your Grace."

"Tell them I promise that once this war is over, I will find them and have them buried in Demetia."

Clyde bowed low. "At once, Your Grace."

Then, he turned and walked out of the tent.

Megolin turned to his page.

"Tell the servants to tear this tent down. And ready our horses."

"Aye, Your Grace," the lad said, then spun around and darted out of the tent.

Megolin turned back to Merlin and Igraine and saw his son's cloak glowing purple.

C.J. BROWN

3

FORGIVENESS

IT WAS TWO HOURS BEFORE the column resumed its march amidst shouting and crying and neighing. The roads were too dangerous and did not provide enough cover for the Demetians, so they walked through the woods, beneath the shade of the canopy.

The hooves of Merlin's mare sucked up mud as it trod forward.

The air was so heavy that Merlin found it difficult to breathe.

Each time he tried to suck in air, it seemed to just crowd his pathway like an army squeezing through a city gate.

His neck was numb and ached at the same time. He

tried moving his head around to get some feeling again, but to no avail.

Fighting to breathe and keep off the damp and cold, Merlin sat silently in his saddle as the mare walked on, flies buzzing around its head.

Every time one landed on Merlin, he shook it off with more anger than disgust.

From behind, he could hear crying babes and sons and daughters mourning their dying fathers.

He turned and spotted the wagon carrying Arthur.

Uther's body had been tightly wrapped with cloth that was packed with some fragrant herbs the foragers found near the camp and had been placed in a box. It was not nearly as fitting as it should have been. Uther Pendragon was one of the greatest men of his time, but more than that, he was loved, missed, and mourned. Megolin had promised Igraine that he would be properly buried when they got to Gilidor, as befitted a Roman general.

Since then, Igraine had not been able to go to him. She could not handle seeing her husband like that.

Megolin had also ordered some of the servants to polish Arthur's armor. His body was pale, and his eyes were sunken, but the spell of containment Merlin had cast upon his soul had stayed his degradation. And after the servants had cleaned his body and armor, he didn't appear too horrid. His hair had been washed and brushed. His face, too, and all the blood was gone. He still wore his armor, and the points where the arrows had breached the iron plate could be seen clearly. The plate itself had been polished and shone with a regal brilliance, and the five dragons of his clan had never stood out more.

Merlin turned back to look ahead, at endless rows upon rows of towering pines clinging to autumn.

He feared there would be more heavy rains soon. Autumn storms were the worst of the year, and then the first snows would fall, and the drenched ground would freeze. Merlin had never had to endure the harshness of winter. Physically, he had spent his entire life in the palace and within the city of Demetia, with roaring hearths to chase away the cold, a roof to keep the rain out, and dry, crisp chambers made of oaken planks that held the warmth of the fire.

Out here, in attire several days' old, with the autumn storms gathering, with Demetia a pile of rubble, burned and looted and occupied by the enemy, and with his heart and mind heavy with grief, misery, anger, and regret, he was a long way from home.

Merlin was shaken from his thoughts when his destrier suddenly neighed, and her legs gave out. They buckled, and she collapsed to the ground, throwing Merlin out of his saddle.

He landed with a thud on the soggy leaves.

Megolin's own horse neighed at the sound as he reined up.

"What happened?" Megolin asked as Merlin got up and dusted some of the leaves off his cloak.

Igraine was looking on as well, and the column too.

Merlin knelt down beside the horse.

"She's carrying too much weight," he said, and started removing the lobstered steel on the horse's neck, when he noticed a part of it was breached.

The metal plates clanged as he moved them, and a foul odor suddenly emerged. That's when he saw the blood.

"She's wounded," he said, throwing the armor aside.

It landed with a loud clang, and a boy from the first row of the column stepped forward. His face was black with soot stains, and he wore a faded leather vest.

"I can look at her, Y'Grace," he said. "Me dad's the stable master at Demetia."

Merlin stood up and let the boy approach.

He knelt by the horse.

Dried blood had caked around the wound, and green pus had already appeared.

"She's wounded bad," the boy said.

He reached for the wound and held something.

Cringing up his face, the destrier suddenly screamed and began to kick with its legs, but the boy did not seem to worry.

His hand flew out suddenly, his fingers bloody.

He was holding a bodkin, capable of piercing even heavy plate. A part of the haft still remained, cracked and fissured.

The stable master's son rose.

"I'm sorry, Y'Grace," he said, "but there ain't nothing

I can do. The infection's already taken hold. We should end her misery. It'd be a mercy. My father always used to end it for the wounded horses when they couldn't be healed."

Merlin looked at the destrier's eyes as it whickered and flailed weakly.

Mergus, Merlin had named her, for one of his predecessors from the elder days of the old kingdom. He had been his companion for ten years now.

With tears in his eyes, he turned to the boy.

"How old are you?"

"Five-and-ten, if it please Y'Grace."

"What's your name?"

"Ryon, Y'Grace, if it please you."

Merlin looked back at Mergus.

"I can save her," he said.

He knelt again beside his friend and placed his hand on her neck.

He closed his eyes as the first rows of the column, the man driving the wagon carrying Arthur, his father, Igraine, and Ryon, looked on.

He muttered something, too quietly for anyone to hear, and then a light began to glow from his palm. A breath of wind gusted between them, rustling the canopy, setting the leaves to swirling, and making Megolin and Igraine's cloaks flap, just as the candles had guttered when he healed Arthur's arrow wound after returning from Pittentrail.

Mergus whickered as his wound began to heal. The

flesh and skin grew to rejoin, and a moment later, Merlin pulled his hand back and stood.

"She'll live now," he said.

"Hey!" Someone shouted at once.

The person was shouldering through the crowd.

"You!" He shouted as he burst out of the column.

His tunic was black with dirt and a few locks of white hair hung over his aged eyes.

Clyde placed a mailed hand on his chest.

"No, it's fine," Merlin said.

Clyde looked menacingly at the man, then moved his hand away.

The old man glared at Merlin, his eyes tearing.

"You could have saved my son!" He yelled. "My little boy…cleaved by the Huns, he was, and died in my arms, he did. 'Papa, I'm afraid,' he kept saying, and what could I do? I would have given anything to bring him back! He died from his wounds because he fought for you!"

He pointed at Merlin.

"And what do I see?" He spat. "You're here healing bloody horses, making sure that there foreigner is alive. Me and many more of us have lost those dear to us. And you didn't do anything to save them."

Merlin looked at him.

A hush had fallen over the woods and the crowd. Everyone was staring at Merlin, and he could feel his head turning light.

Finally, Commander Clyde broke the silence.

"How dare you speak that way to your prince?" He shouted at the man. "It's because of him you're still alive! If it--"

"General...don't...please," Merlin stopped him.

He looked at the old man.

"I promise you, I would have helped, I--"

"What? You didn't know he was injured? The entire bloody lot of us is injured! And you didn't help nobody"

Merlin was about to say something when he turned to Megolin.

"And you!" He shouted. "You lock up the food, thinking we're all thieves. Me brother and I, and all of us," he swept his hand across the crowd, "are starving."

He paused.

Then he turned to Arthur.

"It's because of that foreigner there," he said. "Ever since he's arrived, there's been trouble. First, he brings those savages along, then he goes and insults the north, and now the north is out to crush us for helping him! He brought those barbarians to Demetia. It's because of him that Demetia is burned!"

"Silence!"

The trees rustled as Megolin's voice boomed through the woods, carrying his words far and clear.

Megolin looked at the old man with glaring eyes, angry and grieving.

"That foreigner is my nephew," he said. "Second in

line to the throne, and therefore your lord! Show him some respect!"

The old man looked at him poisonously.

"Maybe he don't need to be my king. I'll just leave. All of you are going to die anyway."

"That's enough," Clyde growled.

He turned to the two Royal Guards standing nearby.

"Arrest this man," he said. "Throw him in the back of a wagon and put him in irons. If he so much as speaks, cut out his tongue."

The two Royal Guards walked up to him and walked him off, holding his arms with an iron grip.

The column parted to let them through, and the man walked off, silent.

When the crowd reformed, they disappeared, and Merlin looked down at the ground.

Mergus was standing by his side, and Ryon beside her.

"Merlin," Megolin said, angrily. "Saddle up. We've stopped for too long."

Merlin turned and placed one foot in the stirrup, then heaved himself up onto the horse.

Megolin wheeled around and started off again, and Merlin snapped his reins, looking at his father.

He was in a red rage, and Merlin could sense that he was struggling to maintain his composure. He was the king, after all, and a king could not show weakness, doubt, rage, or fear.

As the column started moving again, he retrieved his

waterskin and poured some on Mergus' neck, cleaning out the pus and blood with his hand.

When she was clean, he poured a little more on his hand to clean it, and then put the skin away.

But all the while, his mind had been fixed upon the old man.

What he said had hurt Merlin more than he realized words could, but what hurt more was that he knew he was right.

He could have saved the man's son. He could have saved all the wounded that were with them.

"So, I will," he muttered.

"Excuse me, Father," he looked at Megolin. "Aunt."

He reined up, and Megolin and Igraine stopped as well.

"No one but the hunters are allowed to leave the column, Merlin," his father said in a tone that brooked no argument.

"I'm not leaving the column, Father," Merlin answered. "There is something I must do. We need not stop the march again."

Megolin looked at him.

"Fine," he said, brusquely, and turned his horse around to gallop off, going ahead of the column.

Clyde and the Royal Guards galloped after him, but Igraine remained.

"Be careful of your feelings, Merlin," she said. "Do not let hate you consume, nor grief distract from you must do."

She looked at the wagon rattling ahead with Arthur's body.

Merlin looked at him as well.

"I won't," he said.

Igraine turned and galloped away, and the column started moving again, around Merlin.

He looked about him and saw the stable master's son.

"Ryon!" He shouted.

The boy looked at him.

Merlin swung down from his saddle amidst the crowd, and the boy ran over to him.

"Yes, my prince?"

"Don't call me that," he said. "I'm Merlin."

The boy nodded hesitantly.

"Here," Merlin offered him the reins. "Keep an eye on her for me."

Ryon took the reins.

"I will, my—Merlin. I will."

Merlin nodded and turned to see the crowd.

Women and children walked amongst wagons bearing the wounded. They wore bloody bandages around their heads and arms and legs, and many of them seemed asleep.

There were not many carts among them, so many more of the wounded had to hobble along, holding onto friends and family.

One man's face was black and red on the right side, with boils and welts all across. His arm was slung around the neck of a young man with a burly neck and burly arms. His right eye was closed and sealed shut by dry pus, and his scalp was scorched and black, with a chunk of his hair missing.

The burns went all the way down his neck and Merlin couldn't tell if they ended at the collar of his tunic or continued on.

He walked up to him and looked at the big lad.

"What is your name?" He asked.

He stopped, and the burned man's red eye flicked open.

"Henry," the burly lad answered.

"What's his name?" Merlin looked at the man he was helping.

"Mykal," Henry said. "He's my father."

"Mykal," Merlin said to him. "You're going to be alright. I'm going to heal you."

Henry looked at his father.

His half-burnt lips began to move.

Merlin couldn't tell what he was trying to say.

Henry brought his ear close, and then he looked at Merlin.

"He says thank you."

Merlin nodded, then he looked at him.

"Alright, Mykal," Merlin said, "you just have to stand there."

He placed his hand on the man's tunic and closed his eyes.

"Hear me, Gaea," he muttered, too quietly for even

Henry, who was standing right before him, to hear. "For I call unto you not for my own enrichment or benefit, but to ease the pain of another person. Here me, Gaea, for Mykal and his son, and for the soul of a good man."

He opened his eyes and found Henry looking on in awe as his father's wounds healed, as his skin regrew over his face. The blood and ooze were still there, but the wounds were disappearing.

The welts on his scalp all went away, leaving smooth and clear skin.

Merlin retrieved his waterskin and a silver-embroidered handkerchief. He soaked the cloth with some of the water and used it to wipe away the blood and crust from the older man's person.

When it was done, Mykal blinked and looked at him.

"Thank you," he said. "Thank you."

"What can we do to repay you?" Henry asked him.

"Just keep believing," he said.

Henry straightened.

He nodded.

Merlin turned to the next wounded he saw.

The boy was a little lad, no more than ten-and-two. He had a great gash in his upper arm that was bandaged with a bloody cloth.

Merlin removed it and healed the wound within seconds.

He and his mother thanked him and then Merlin moved onto the next wounded person. Her arm was suspended from her neck and Merlin could see the spot where the blade had been driven through her shoulder.

He went up to her. The blade hadn't gone all the way through it seemed, and there was no infection. It was not as bad as some of the other wounds that he could see, but he healed it all the same, and moved on.

By nightfall that day, the column had covered ten miles, and Merlin had healed a thousand people.

He was a long way from the head of the column when the sentries flanking the column forwarded the order to halt amidst the gathering darkness.

As wagon-drivers unhitched their horses and tethered them, and those who had been walking sank onto the ground with relief, Merlin turned and walked toward one of the soldiers. He carried a spear and boasted a leather vest embroidered with the crest of the Megolin clan, and a chainmail hauberk.

"Where is the prisoner?" Merlin asked him.

"In that wagon, my prince," he said, pointing.

Merlin looked and saw the old man shackled to an iron ring in the floor of the wagon.

He set off towards him.

As he walked, the people around him set up their tents.

Megolin still didn't allow any fires, so the darkness was almost hindering, but Merlin and all the others acclimated soon enough.

The wounded lay on the ground with their eyes closed as the less injured or younger ones set up the pavilions.

People started lining up to collect their supper from the baggage train. Baggage master Royce had let the bread dry for the first few hours of the day, so now it wasn't as soggy as it had been at dawn. So, Merlin saw people walking away with pewter plates of bread and some other things.

He turned and headed to the food carts to ask for one.

The old man scooped some bread out of one bag, a few slices of cheese from another, and some roast meat from the boar the hunters had brought back that morning.

Merlin walked away with the plate and towards the wagon where the old man had been shackled.

The man's eyes flicked open at the sound of his approach and locked onto his own eyes that glowed yellow.

"My prince," he said. As he moved, the links of his chains rattled and clinked.

Merlin stopped before him. "I brought you food," he said, holding out the plate.

The man didn't say anything. He didn't even move.

From the rest of the column, they could hear the people downing their supper like famished beasts.

Then a human voice broke the sounds of the woods.

"My son is dead," he said. "My home, burned and looted by barbarians. And I lost me wife years ago, so why should I keep on living?"

Merlin looked at him. "Because you are still on this earth," he said. "Because you are part of something far larger than any of us."

The old man's chains rattled as he moved again. "I don't care about any of that," he said. "I just want my son back."

Silence hung between them once more, until the old man said, "But I'll never get him back."

Merlin placed the plate of food on the wagon and turned to the guard standing beside it.

"Release him," he ordered.

The man turned to the side of the wagon, his ring of keys jingling. Then he tried the first one, then the second. When he turned the third one, the lock clicked, and the man's chains fell away and clattered onto the oak planks.

The old man rubbed his wrists and looked at Merlin.

"Why are you freeing me?" He said.

"Because being a grieving father is no crime. I admit, I could have saved your son, and I didn't, and that he will never return to us. But he is not gone, not truly. His spirit remains, and for him, and for the woman you loved, you must fight this war."

"What war?" The old man said. "We've already lost."

"No," Merlin said. "That foreigner you were speaking of...is Arthur Pendragon, the one the sorcerers of old predicted would reunite the Isle and return peace to Britannia."

"Huns are here," the old man said. "Demetia is burned. The north marches on all of us. We'd be fools to trust prophecies and the like."

"This isn't some legend," Merlin said. "Arthur is the

chosen one. He doesn't know it yet. But he is. And this war is not between Highlanders and Demetians, or even Britons against Huns. It's about light and dark. And we will stand for the light, and Gaea curse us all who stand by and watch the shadow of evil fall upon the world."

Merlin paused.

"Your son is still alive," Merlin said. "His soul lives on, just as the soul of every other who ascends to the Starhearth. I say again, for him and the woman you loved, you must fight, because the light is what they stood for. I'll leave you to your supper."

4

CORNERED

MERLIN DIDN'T RETURN TO HIS father's tent that night, but communicated to him that he would be staying where he was.

Seated amongst his people, Merlin forced himself to eat. Thankfully, it didn't taste as foul as the water he had drunk the day before. Merlin felt somewhat comforted by that. It was proof that he was failing less. But regardless, the bile was still there, the bile of Arthur's death, and the fate of the Isle that hung in the balance.

It hangs in my hands, Merlin thought.

Merlin knew Arthur would fulfill his destiny and bring peace and unity to the Isle, but he could not do that while he was dead, which only Merlin could reverse. And yet he was failing.

When the ordeal that was supper was over, he laid out his bedroll and lay down, staring up at the canopy of the pine trees with his glowing, yellow eyes.

"Tell me, Gaea," he prayed. "How do I bring him back? How do I heal his soul?"

Merlin remembered what Arthur had looked like when he met with him in Starhearth, what he had said.

I am done with that world...nothing but grief and pain...all is lost...all is lost...

Those words sounded ten times over in the confines of his mind, then a hundred times more, keeping him from sleep.

And when he did manage to catch some rest, the nightmare returned.

This time, Merlin could see an entire battlefield. Demetian, Caledonian, Rodwinian, and Astavonian banners, and the standards of all the other great clans of the Isle and the lesser ones as well, had all fallen. Some were anchored in the ground. One Demetian banner, its purple field scarred black by fire and dirt, hung from the haft that stood up diagonally from the ground.

Suddenly, flakes began to drift past his face.

Snow, he thought at first, but then he looked down and saw the flakes that had caked upon his sandals.

Ash.

Around him, small fires were burning. Wounded men,

their hands and faces bloody and soot-stained, begged for mercy. And then Merlin saw the trees all around. They were all burning. The green leaves had all but burned away, and the withering barks spit and cracked as red embers swirled around them.

And then Merlin heard a horn, a far-off and low roar, guttural and monstrous, like the growl of some ancient and terrible beast.

Merlin found himself stirring, and caught glimpses of the canopy above him, but still the sound of the horn lingered. Only now it was much louder and of a far higher register.

Its call echoed through the trees for a great many seconds, when Merlin's eyes flicked open, and he bolted up.

"Huns," he said, his breath misting before him.

He jumped up.

"Wake up!" He shouted. "All of you! Wake up!"

At once, people began stirring, and once they heard the horn, they jolted up and started running about frantically.

Merlin looked around. The sky was turning a dark blue to the east. The sun would be upon them soon. If the Huns were smart, they would attack from the west. During the day, getting their enemy to face the sun would have been the best strategy to attack a mass of wounded refugees, most of whom weren't soldiers, but at night, darkness was their friend.

They would attack from the west, Merlin realized.

But, that means they're right before us. Somehow, they got ahead. We'd be marching right into them.

"Prince Merlin!" He heard someone shout.

He turned to see a Royal Guard ahorse.

"His Grace commands you to return to the front. The Huns are here!

"Sir!" Merlin yelled as he ran over, "we need to change direction. If the Huns are attacking from the west, these people will be marching right into them!"

"His Grace has seen to that!" The Guard bellowed. "Now we must get to the front!"

Merlin held the saddle and swung up behind the Royal Guard.

The man wheeled the horse around beside the column as other Guards turned the people north.

He snapped the reins, and the garron galloped off, neighing, kicking up mud and leaves with its iron hooves.

The horns had gone silent now, but shouts and screams and the far-off clangor of steel had replaced them.

As they drew near to the site of battle, plunging towards the still dark side of the world, Merlin glimpsed steel swords and maces crashing down on oaken shields painted with the colors of Demetia. Men were shouting and screaming, and Merlin spotted Verovingian standing nearby, his devotions glowing blue. He held a greatsword, with blood splattered across its side.

He turned to see Merlin fly off the saddle, his cloak billowing and roll in the dirt as the Royal Guard charged on, his sword drawn, and slashed at the first barbarian soldier as he reached their ranks.

Merlin jumped up, his hands and face splattered with mud, and drew his weapon. He ran towards Verovingian, who followed him, and he slashed at one of the Huns.

The magic of the sword flowed through his veins and paralyzed the barbarian, leaving him alive but motionless on the ground.

He hacked at another, shearing through his fur skin cloak, but stopping when the blade met his skin. Then he slashed.

The Huns were shrieking and howling, and one charged at him with his great ax held high.

Merlin jumped aside just as the weapon swung and slashed the barbarian warrior's arm.

He fell like a bag of stones, dropping his weapon.

Merlin looked around him.

The Royal Guards were doing most of the fighting now. Their force of three hundred men had been at the back of the column, and were not here to help with the fight. But fifty Royal Guards were better than a hundred regular soldiers, even cavalry, and Merlin was certain they'd at least be able to hold out till the main force arrived.

He searched for his father, looking here and there, trying to hear his voice if it was there to be heard.

Slashing at Huns and cutting his way through the chaotic scene, he found neither army was fighting as one anymore. Each Demetian was fighting single combat with a Hun, struggling to stay alive.

Merlin saw an ax crash through the oaken shield of one of the Royal Guards.

It had nearly struck his head.

Merlin ran towards the Hun as he growled and snarled, trying to wrench his blade free of the Demetian's shield, and slashed his side.

The man's eyes widened, and then he fell over, sending the Royal Guard staggering back when he let go of the ax.

The knight nodded at him and left to continue fighting.

Within moments, Merlin turned at the sound of the three hundred soldiers thundering towards them, swords drawn, their cloaks rippling and armor glinting from the light of the rising sun.

Merlin jumped aside and they collided with the Hun ranks, splitting their force in two.

By the time the sun was completely above the horizon, the Hun army had been dispersed and the ones who survived were falling back.

Merlin stood on the field of battle, surrounded by fallen Huns. Nestled on the carpet of leaves, the ground was littered with bloody weapons and splintered shields.

His own blade was lined with the blood of the Huns, but he had not killed anyone.

Demetian soldiers walked about, checking to see if any of the Huns lying on the ground were still alive.

"Merlin!" He heard his father bellow.

He turned to see him standing a few yards away, his armor and cloak splattered with blood and mud.

He walked up to him.

"Father," he greeted him.

Megolin's face looked as fierce as an autumn storm, dark and brooding as it was.

"I'll be holding a council meeting. I wish for you to attend."

Merlin knew his father was in no mood for argument right now, so he decided he would just comply.

"As you wish, Father," he said.

They walked together back to the king's pavilion. The purple tent had been splattered with blood and fallen Huns and Demetians alike lay around it.

Merlin stopped when he realized that the Royal Guard lying face-up beside a Hun, his eyes staring blankly at the sky, was the same one who had sent for him when the battle began.

Merlin clenched his jaw, then turned to walk into the tent.

Igraine was sitting by the fire, watching the flames twitch and snap as the pine logs and twigs spit and cracked.

Megolin sat at the trestle table, his helm resting on the planks, his whitening hair tousled and hung over his face.

Merlin walked over and sat opposite to him.

He looked around the tent.

Nothing had been disturbed, which meant none of the Huns had managed to get in.

Clyde shook Merlin out of his thoughts when he sauntered through the tent flaps, his face dotted with sweat.

Merlin noticed he was bleeding from his upper arm. The blood had soaked his cloak, turning the purple a dark red, and a line of blood trailed down to his hand.

"My lady, are you alright?" he asked Igraine.

She looked at him and smiled sadly.

"I am, and I thank you for your consideration."

"You're wounded," Megolin noted, looking at the trail of blood along the general's arm.

"It's nothing, Your Grace," he answered. "And no, Merlin, I do not want you to heal me."

Merlin smiled a solemn, lop-sided smile as baggage master Royce appeared, as well as the Commander of the Royal Guard.

Royce's forehead looked like wax with all the sweat he was producing, and his face was pale and pasty.

They all seated themselves around the table, but Igraine remained by the fire.

"How many men did we lose?" Megolin asked Clyde.

"We don't know yet, Your Grace. My men are still counting."

"Were any of the people hurt?" Merlin said, anxiously.

"I hope not," Clyde answered. "But some definitely were. We also don't know how many or if their wounds were fatal."

Megolin turned to Royce.

"Do we still have our supplies?"

The baggage master licked his lips.

"Y-yes, Your Grace. It was good fortune that the Huns did not attempt to raid our stores."

"They would have," Clyde said.

"Commander Raymon, how many Royal Guards did we lose?"

"Eighteen, Your Grace," the old man said.

A line of blood had dried, trailing from his brow to his cheek and reflected the orange flames as if it were a fire spear launched from a Roman scorpion.

"They all died with honor, Your Grace."

"I am sure," Megolin responded. "We will bury them at sunset, after another day's march. It's not like that the Huns will attack us again after we defeated their force. Still, we cannot take any chances. How many were there?"

"We couldn't see for sure," Clyde answered, frowning, "but our best guess is there were at least two hundred of them. Based on how many we saw run off, I'd say we killed the lot of 'em."

Megolin nodded.

"We can't afford another attack," he said. "Clyde, I want you to reform the defense. Split your men up. I want the civilians surrounded. And search among them for young and able lads who can fight. We need all the arms we can get."

"Aye, Your Grace," Clyde said.

Megolin turned to Igraine.

"Do you have anything to add?" He asked.

They all looked at her, and she kept gazing at the fire.

Then she turned to Megolin.

"Your plan is sound," she said. "But I suggest me might double our speed. Place the wounded on the horses, and the cavalry can march on foot. Like that, I should think we'll arrive at Gilidor sometime tonight."

Clyde turned back to Megolin.

"I agree," he said. "It can be done."

Megolin nodded.

And then he rose.

Merlin stood up with the rest.

"See these things done. We march at once."

The three men bowed and turned to leave the tent.

Once they had left, Megolin sat again and turned to his son.

"Word is you were healing the wounded folk yesterday…and that you freed the man who shouted at you and threatened desertion."

Merlin nodded.

Megolin looked at him for a moment.

"That was a good thing," he finally remarked. "Mercy and fairness are the traits of a wise king."

"I don't want to be king," Merlin said.

"No, you don't. But that doesn't mean you can't have the traits of a wise one. And along with doing the right thing, you have gained the support of the people. They are grateful to you and will stand by you as true friends for all of time."

Merlin nodded.

"I want you to continue doing that. Heal the wounded, all of them."

Merlin felt doubt throw its ugly shadow upon his heart, but he pushed it aside.

"I will, Father."

He stood and turned to Igraine.

"And I will bring my cousin back as well."

Then he turned and walked out of the tent.

Outside, the fallen were already being cleared.

The Huns were being placed side by side, and soldiers were piling soil onto them. They may have been barbaric savages who had taken everything from them, but Demetians were not vengeful or spiteful creatures. No matter how vile they were, they were still living beings, and Gaea did not differentiate between nationalities and creeds. And, sadly, until such time as other peoples didn't differentiate among each other, Demetia would have to keep fighting.

As the Huns disappeared from sight, the Demetian soldiers built pyres for their own fallen.

Merlin searched everywhere for someone wounded.

He found one soldier, leaning beside a wagon. His cloak was dark and soaked with blood, and his right arm ended at the stump where his elbow once was.

He was unconscious, with mud and blood smeared across his face, but he was breathing.

Merlin knelt beside him and held his arm.

The wind rose and the leaves fluttered, and the man jolted awake, panicking, but Merlin calmed him, and he watched as flesh and bone and skin began to regrow from his elbow.

But then Merlin felt himself weakening and he let go.

The man eyed his arm. The stump was healed, and rather than being at his elbow, it was halfway to his wrist.

"I'm sorry," he said. "I will get back to you and you will have the rest of your arm."

But the man didn't seem to worry that he hadn't regained his hand.

"Thank you, my prince. Thank you," he said.

Merlin helped him to his feet and then left to heal another.

Most of the wounded were soldiers. A few were Royal Guards, and Merlin was relieved to find that he had not encountered any civilians yet. But he dared not hope for too much.

As Merlin moved through the column, amidst shouting and neighing, groups of soldiers ran along the side every now and then, headed to their new posts.

By the time Merlin got halfway through the column, they were marching again. Merlin found a few wounded civilians, all of them old men and young lads who'd tried to fight. He healed all of them and kept on moving.

He had been healing them so quickly that by the time he had reached the point where he had stopped yesterday, the sun was only just passing its zenith.

Merlin tried to find the old man whose son had died from the battle with the Huns at Demetia.

He found him sitting on a horse, a bloody bandage wrapped around his side.

He reined up when he spotted Merlin.

"Was near done for," he said. "Would have been if I wasn't patched up when I was."

"Thank you," Merlin said, "for fighting."

The man looked at him. "My son did the same."

A moment of silence went by, and then Merlin reached up and placed a hand on his arm and closed his eyes.

When the wind calmed a few moments later, and the leaves settled once more, Merlin opened his eyes to see the old man looking at his bloody bandage.

He started unwrapping it.

He threw the cloth down and lifted his tunic to see skin where his wound had been, unscarred.

He looked back at Merlin.

"Thank you," he said. "Thank you."

"It is Gaea you should thank," Merlin responded, "for it is Gaea's powers that flow through me, as they flow through any warlock."

The old man bowed his head.

"I will see you again, my prince," he said.

He looked behind and saw a wounded young lad with a bloody bandage around his head.

Merlin started walking towards him.

"No," the old man said.

Merlin turned to look at him.

"Forgive me, my prince, but I want to help him. His wounds are not fatal. And they're not like to get corrupted. The soldiers said give the horses to the wounded. That lad there is wounded. Please, I want to do this."

Merlin eyed him.

Then he smiled and nodded.

The old man nodded back, then snapped the reins and trotted off toward the boy.

He swung down from his saddle, said a few words to him, and then the old man and woman standing beside him began to weep as he helped their son up.

Merlin smiled and went to find another wounded fellow.

That night, Merlin did not stay with the people. Instead, he walked through the camp, back to the front, where Arthur was.

The little tents that the people had set up for themselves were placed between the trees and beside old trunks that held back the worst of the winds. Megolin had meant to keep marching, but they would not be able to with droves of rain lashing them and howling winds that threatened to freeze them. Because of the cover of the storm, Megolin had also permitted small fires in every tent. He was hoping the Huns were far behind and would be held back by the rain. And if they were somehow to get near, the deluge would be too heavy for them to see much.

As he walked, his yellow eyes looking ahead, he looked up at the sound of thunder and the sudden flash of lightning.

The wind began to howl, pulling at the balding branches and snapping the smaller twigs.

The leaves across the ground began to swirl and flutter, and the air turned cold.

As Merlin walked, the wind set his cloak to billowing, and Merlin felt a pang of relief. Whenever a warlock healed a wound, the winds would pick up. The accounts also said that when the warlocks of old revived someone, a great storm would always gather as the person's soul returned to his person. Merlin chose to see this as an omen, an omen that Arthur was about to return.

He got to the front of the column an hour later, by which point the rains were falling heavily and the woods resounded with the sound of a million drops battering the leaves on the ground. The gales howled between the barks like the wailing of a great beast, mournful and terrible.

The wind was sending the rain into Merlin's eyes, but he shielded them as best he could, and kept his sights on Arthur's glowing form.

The blue light shined through even the little canopy that had been built over the wagon to keep most of the water out.

With confidence, Merlin walked up to the wagon and removed the tarp.

The purple cloth covering him turned a dark maroon at once as the rains drenched it.

When Merlin uncovered his cousin's face, his hair was already soaked.

Merlin froze at the sight of Arthur.

His eyes had sunken. His skin was pale, paler than ice, and his lips had formed straight, mean line.

Merlin shook the sudden shock away and placed his hand on Arthur's shoulder. Merlin opened his eyes to find himself standing amidst Starhearth once more. The souls of millions shone from afar as he looked around.

"Arthur!" Merlin yelled.

His voice echoed through the endless, groundless world.

"Arthur…Arthur…Arthur!…Arthur!"

But for a long while, Arthur did not appear.

Dread began to creep into his heart, heavy and suffocating.

He found himself fighting to breathe.

"Calm down," he told himself. "I need to focus. Arthur is depending on me. My father is depending on me. My aunt is depending upon me. Everyone is. I need to bring Arthur back."

"Arthur!" He yelled again, and the echoes carried his words to the farthest corners of the afterworld. "I need you to listen to me! You have to return! Britannia is falling apart! The North marches on the rest of the isle. The Huns have burned Demetia. They've burned the land. Land's End is the only place that hasn't been affected by the fighting. We're heading there. But Land's End will not stay safe forever. Some of the other lords have been defeated and imprisoned by the Huns. The rest are preparing to flee. Everything is breaking apart, Arthur. Your mother misses you. She mourns your father. And you are the only one who can make things right. You are the only one who can make sure that we survive. You are the only one who can make sure your father didn't die for nothing."

Arthur appeared at once, glaring at Merlin. "What do you think I could possibly do?" he snapped. "I failed. I lost. I tried talking to the other lords, and they all wanted to run. It was foolish of me to think we could fight. We should all have run. If you mean to not die, I suggest you get ships, and leave this wretched island behind."

Merlin could not believe what he was hearing. "Arthur," he pleaded, "you cannot do this. You cannot abandon your people!"

"They are not my people," he said, shaking his head. "I have no people. I am an exile of Rome, and a stranger in Britannia. And even if they were my people, there is nothing I can do to help them. I died once. I lost. If you bring me back, nothing will change."

Merlin looked at him. "Arthur," he said, quietly, "I know you're in pain. I do not know myself what kind of pain you are suffering through, but I can tell you that we will be there for each other. We will all be there to help you. But you must allow me to bring you back. You are supposed to…you are…you are meant to bring back the old kingdom. You are meant to right the wrongs that the last king committed. You are meant to bring peace and unity back to the Isle, to end our wars and turmoil. You must do this."

Arthur shook his head. "There is no pain here," he said. "Here, I can speak with my father. I can speak with Olivie. But, you go on and live. Sail for the uncharted lands, like I said. It should be peaceful there. I am done with fighting, Merlin. Goodbye."

And then he disappeared.

Merlin's eyes flicked open.

The rains were still pouring, and the thunder and lightning continued to roar and light up the sky.

Merlin looked at Arthur.

He still glowed blue, and though there was light before him, the world had never been darker for Merlin.

5

SPELLS

ORNING FOUND THE WARLOCK PRINCE huddled by the charred embers of his fire, as the storm finally abated outside.

He had not slept, nor rested. All he could think about was the doom that had befallen the world. The sunlight that pierced the lightening clouds and drifted through the tent felt overwhelming and only reminded Merlin that the end was near.

The tent flaps behind him flew open, but Merlin did not hear anything till the man said, "His Grace requests your presence."

Merlin did not respond. He did not even look at the speaker.

The lad walked up to him. "My prince?"

Still, he did not respond.

"Merlin?" he asked. Everyone knew that the prince of Demetia did not like being called that, but calling the prince anything but the prince was difficult for most. Sometimes even Megolin forgot that Merlin preferred to separate himself from the worldly realm of kingdoms and thrones.

Merlin blinked, and thought he heard something. He turned to find his father's page standing beside him.

"Merlin," he said, "the king is requesting your presence."

Merlin nodded, almost not hearing him. He rose. "Thank you," he said, then turned and walked out of the tent, followed by the page.

Two guards were standing outside.

"Have this tent packed away," Merlin told them. "We'll be marching soon."

"At once, my prince," one of them muttered.

Merlin and Henry left them and went over to the tent beside his.

Megolin was seated at the trestle table with Igraine.

"Your Grace," the page said when they appeared at the flaps.

Megolin rose. He noticed his son's look. "Are you alright?" he asked him.

Merlin looked at him for a moment. "It's Arthur."

Megolin looked at the page. "Leave us," he said.

"Your Grace." He bowed his head, then turned and left.

"He's what we're talking about," Megolin said to Merlin. "When can he return?"

Merlin looked at him regretfully. "I—I…"

"What's wrong?" Igraine asked.

"I don't know," Merlin muttered.

"What do you mean?" Megolin asked him.

"He is changed, Father. He is suffering. He doesn't want to return. He's found his father and Olivie there."

He paused.

"He says there is no fight to be fought, and that we should depart for the West. He says we'll be able to find some uncharted land and escape there from the horrors of this world. I have tried telling him everything that's going on. I have tried communicating to him the danger that has befallen the Isle and that he needs to return if the light is to continue shining."

Igraine looked at Merlin. "Healing a broken man is like reforging a broken sword. You don't fuse the two pieces back together. That would leave the point where they had broken weak. You'd have to melt down the entire thing and forge it anew. Arthur is the broken blade. You cannot pressure him to return. He must let go of the old world, the old things. The destiny he was chosen for was never certain until we sailed from Paris. But now that destiny will happen, sure as the sun will rise. You must not lose faith, Merlin. Good always outweighs the bad, and it will not fail us now."

Merlin looked at her. "I will try, but…"

"I don't think there's room for that," Megolin said. "I don't want to pressure you, son, but time is a highly precious commodity that we have dangerously little of now. You must hurry."

Merlin looked at his father for a moment, thinking. "I will not fail you. Arthur will return, and by his own will." He turned and left the tent.

The people were already packing away their tents. The fog bank was clearing, and the ground was a puddled, mushy landscape.

Merlin's shoes caked with mud, and his cloak picked up dirt as he walked across to where the wagon was.

Just then, Verovingian appeared beside the cart with his horse.

"No, thank you, friend," Merlin told him. "I'm going to be here. Reviving Arthur is going to take a great deal more than asking him to return. Lend my horse to someone who needs it."

Verovingian nodded. "I didn't see you before because I never had the chance," he said. "But I heard about everything you did. Healing the wounded. Freeing the old man who shouted at you before all of Demetia."

"He grieves for his son," Merlin told him. "He did nothing wrong."

"You would be an honorable king," Verovingian told

him. "Sadly, the way the world works is that the honorable often get killed trying to do the right thing and the corrupt go on, winning thrones and crowns."

"That is why my father is king," Merlin said. "He knows how to be honorable and manage the dishonorable at the same time. The successor he appoints will do the same. But governing is far from what my role is."

"Truly spoken. What will you do now?"

"Arthur is suffering," he said. "I am the only one right now who can bring him back. And he needs to return, Verovingian. He must. I keep trying to tell him what will happen if he does not return to fight, to fulfill his destiny. But he does not want to. I don't blame him. Starhearth is a great deal more peaceful. But we cannot abandon this worldly realm to the darkness."

Verovingian thought for a moment. "Might I suggest, rather than telling Arthur more bad things, why don't you tell him the good that will happen if he returns?"

Merlin looked at him. "I'd never thought of that before. I will try it."

He climbed up and sat beside Arthur as those who had already packed up their stuff were standing nearby, ready to begin walking again.

"I will see you again, my friend," Verovingian said, and turned to leave.

For the half hour that elapsed until the march continued, Merlin spent his time remembering all the spells and chants he'd learned while training to be a warlock. All of them were simple things, but none of them were at all substantial regarding someone's revival and their return from Starhearth.

Spells were tools that warlocks used so that a goal beyond their ability could be achieved. Spells were thus dangerous. They could be used by ill souls who sought to corrupt the world for their own gain. Only the wisest warlocks knew spells, for only the wisest could be trusted to know what they were meant for, and not use them for anything else.

Merlin's grandfather had not been around when he was born as a warlock, so there had been no other warlock to train him. So, he trained himself, reading the books of the ancient sorcerers, practicing for hours amidst the eternal sentinels that formed the enchanted wood. His father and those with devotions were the closest he had to tutors. Megolin believed that Merlin would be worthy of learning the spells, and so Merlin learned them. The Demetians secretly doubted their king's decision, and Merlin did not blame them. Spells were used by corrupt minds for bad. And they could sometimes corrupt even the good minds that were weak.

Merlin remembered the first spell he learned.

It was called, "Earthly summoner, here I am, heed my call and remember my debt.

It was a simple spell. One who had not yet learned how to control the wind and the oceans could use it to do so.

Merlin had felt so afraid, so worried that he was standing at the start of a dark path.

The night before he trained with spells, he dreamt that he was standing at a fork in the road. One path was flanked by orchards and flowers and was fresh and bright. The other was flanked by withering hedges and gnarled trees, haunted and mean. The road was littered with fallen leaves, and it was dark, and the air was strangely uncomfortable.

Yet he had found himself walking that way.

He had started to shout and call for help and try and stop and turn back, but his legs betrayed him, and he just kept drifting further form the light.

That morning, he told his father his dream and pleaded not to learn the spells.

Megolin told him that his fear was justified, and, if anything, should have been encouraging, because the fact that he had feared turning dark meant that he did not want to. So, Megolin had told him to learn the spells and to be aware of himself.

It had been twenty years since then, and Merlin had learned more spells than he could care to remember.

All of them were of an ancient language. No longer spoken by either the commoners or the nobles, it was a language reserved by the warlocks and which survived through them.

He remembered the one for reviving souls that had drifted away.

Many times, he had trained himself by reviving mice that had died just moments before. A spell of containment was only meant for beings who would not return for some time. But if a warlock could revive them immediately, no such spell was required.

Merlin was good at reviving rats and birds, but he had never revived a person before.

He looked at Arthur and could feel the dread and pain he was suffering from.

He closed his eyes and chanted an ancient phrase. Like when he had called upon Gaea to contain Arthur's spirit, he called again to bring him back. But this time, he called upon the universe with all the strength and energy he had. Multiplying the power of the spell, his words carried beyond the din of the march and rose up to the heavens.

Merlin closed his eyes, and when he opened them, he found himself standing amidst the stars of Starhearth, and Arthur was before him.

"What are you doing?" he shouted at him.

"You must return," Merlin said. "You are the chosen one. With your rule, Britannia will survive this war. Britannia will unite, and our people will prosper!"

"You fool!" Arthur bellowed. "I just want to remain here."

Merlin could feel Arthur fighting him.

"Arthur! Listen to sense. You know it's the right thing to return to the world."

"No! I am here! I am at peace! Leave me be!"

A blinding wave of light shone from Arthur's form, and Merlin had to shield his eyes, and then the light dimmed, and he looked to see Arthur gone.

He opened his eyes again as the wagon rattled on.

The people were walking nearby, rank upon rank of them, all of them hoping their leaders would win this war and save Demetia from extinction.

C.J. BROWN

6

COUNSEL

MERLIN FELT LIKE HE COULD not join his father for their afternoon meal. The sting of his failure was still too great. So, he dined with Verovingian.

Megolin did not permit any stops during the day, so they ate either ahorse or afoot from pewter plates, with waterskins at their sides. The midday meal was a combination of cheese, bread, and salted boar.

Verovingian remained atop his horse and Merlin walked beside him.

"Why are you not with your father?" Verovingian asked him.

Merlin chewed a bit of his cheese.

"I have failed," he said. "My father cannot see me now. Not until I have brought Arthur back."

"Distancing yourself from those who support you will not help you."

"No," Merlin said, "but at least I won't have to be so burdened by the shame."

"You will find no such worries with your family," Verovingian answered, finishing the last of his salted boar. "But you will find help and direction."

"You know, I wonder how you were not born a warlock," Merlin said. "You speak like one of the wise ones."

"My prince is most kind," Verovingian said, storing his plate away. He reached for his waterskin which hung from his saddle.

"You must drink as well," he told Merlin.

"I have failed," Merlin answered. "So, the water is foul."

"I am no warlock," Verovingian said, "but one thing I have learned is that if you are destined to fail, everything will feel terrible. Everything will be terrible. Sometimes, things may seem good, but they're actually not. But when you are destined to triumph, everything will be as it should. Forgive me, Merlin, but I would say that you are committed enough--"

Merlin's eyes snapped to him. "What did you say? You think I'm not committed enough? You think I'm standing here, with my people threatened with doom, with everything burning and falling away, and knowing that Arthur needs to return to fix everything, and yet I'm not committed enough to bringing him back?"

Verovingian looked at him. "Merlin, you misunderstand me. I do not mean you are less committed than you can be. I mean you are not committed enough."

Merlin looked at him. "So, you're saying I need to be more committed. How might I do that?"

"You must realize that we do control things to a certain point, but beyond that, we can do no more than act, and hope that our actions will affect things. What you can control is telling Arthur the reasons he should return. Do not use spells. Do not force him. If he returns when he does not want to, he will fall forever to the dark. It will only make things worse. Tell Arthur why he should return, and then let him decide to."

Merlin thought for a moment. "How do you know that's even possible? You haven't spoken to him, haven't heard his words, haven't seen his look of hopelessness and grief and anger. I have, and I don't know what to do."

Verovingian smiled sadly. "There are many things we do not know," he said. "But we must be willing to trust every once in a while, that the universe will not fail us."

"You say that so surely."

"And, I admit, I once did not. But many things have proven me wrong. Please, try this at least."

"We don't have the time."

"There will be time enough if it is to happen," Verovingian promised him.

Then he snapped his reins and went ahead, leaving Merlin to think.

7

HOPE

MERLIN CONSIDERED WHAT Verovingian had told him as he returned to Arthur's wagon. He sat beside him once more and looked at him.

Verovingian had said he essentially just had to set Arthur on the path to healing, and let the rest happen by itself.

It was the kind of thing he knew wiser warlocks would say, but Merlin found it difficult to believe. For one thing, they did not have the time to just let things happen, and for another, how could they even be sure?

All around him, the people marched on, quiet, with all that remained of their worldly possessions either on their backs or borne by the wagons a few of them were lucky to have escaped with. As the Royal Guard formed a shield around Megolin, Igraine, and himself, Merlin tried to steel his resolve.

He believed it was not reliable, what Verovingian had said, but he could think of nothing else, and it wouldn't hurt to take a leap of faith.

So, Merlin closed his eyes and transported himself to Starhearth once more.

"Arthur!" Merlin shouted, and then the entire world was echoing his voice.

A moment went by, and Arthur did not appear.

"Arthur!" Merlin yelled again. "I am not here to tell you to return! I just want to talk!"

A few moments went by, and Merlin started to feel despair. If Arthur didn't want to speak to him, how could they communicate?

Merlin could not give up. "Arthur! I just want to talk!" he yelled again.

A minute went by, and then Arthur appeared before him.

Merlin felt relief douse the fires of his dread.

"Arthur…how are you?"

Arthur looked at him suspiciously.

"Better than I have ever been," he said.

"I've seen this place," Merlin told him. "But I don't think I truly understand it."

"You wouldn't," Arthur said, seeming to smile now.

"But I can tell you about this place the best I can. Olivie calls this place the Soul Field. My father, Uther, because he's Roman, calls this Heaven. What do you call it?"

"Starhearth."

Arthur nodded.

"A just name. But everybody's names for it are born of their culture and religion. If I could name it, I would name it Peace Keep. Because it is peaceful here. No one is fighting. There are no enemies here. There's no running from a usurper or combating hateful barbarians. There's just family who you thought you'd never see again."

Merlin smiled sadly.

"That sounds...yes, peaceful."

Arthur nodded. "You know that we're all going to end up here, right?" he said. "Whether you lose to the Huns, or to the northerners, or they lose, we all end up here. It's clear now that the universe does not discriminate between creeds and religions, and that we're all one, so we'll all be here."

"Yes," Merlin agreed, "but the worldly realm is not just about the survival of your person. It is about the world itself, the light and the dark, the legacy that we leave behind."

"Merlin, I know you hope, but hope is a more dangerous thing than even the worst weapons. Because hope makes things seem right, seem like it will all be all right. And then your hopes are crushed by the weight of defeat and tragedy. There is no point to it. All of you, everyone, will be here one day, and we can all live peacefully then."

Merlin fought to control the despair and loss he was enduring just then.

"Do you really mean that?"

Arthur nodded. "I had hope once," he said. "I had hope that my father would wrest the imperial throne back from the usurper, that Rome would rise once more as the standard of morals and justice that Rome once was, that all the corruption and suffering would be washed away, and that a new and better life awaited not just us, but all of Rome. My grandfather, he wanted to reestablish connections with Britannia, not as rulers, but as friends. My own father had plans to establish true peace throughout the Continent, to end the wars with the barbarians, to end...to end all our troubles. And then...well, you know what happened."

Merlin looked down. "Have you spoken to anyone else besides your father and Olivie?"

"No," Arthur said. "I don't know anyone else who's here."

"Can I speak to them?"

"I think so..." Arthur said. "Do I call them, or do you call them?"

"You call them."

"Father!" Arthur shouted. "Olivie!"

At once, they appeared beside him.

"Merlin," Uther greeted him. "It is good to see you."

"It is," Olivie said.

Merlin looked at them. "Olivie, please forgive me. We could not save you."

"There is nothing to forgive," she said. "After all, you were not the one who loosed that arrow. And now I'm here, with Arthur."

"Merlin," Uther said, "how is Igraine?"

Merlin hesitated. He didn't know whether saying the truth was the right thing now.

But, he realized, it could help with getting Arthur to decide to return from the afterlife. If Uther and Olivie decided to add their voices to his, it could change his mind.

"Aunt Igraine grieves," Merlin said. "For you and her son. But she remains strong. She is an unofficial member of my father's council now. She keeps to herself, to contain her grief."

Uther bowed his head. "Why are you here?" he asked.

"No!" Arthur shouted, and everyone looked at him. "You will not bring this up with them! You will not!"

"What are you talking about?" Uther asked him.

Arthur reduced his volume. "It's nothing, Father. It's just something Merlin didn't want to tell you."

"Arthur, don't do this," Merlin said. "They must know."

"No!" Arthur yelled.

"Arthur Pendragon!" Uther shouted. "You are my son still, and you will not stop me from asking a question and receiving an answer! I want Merlin to tell me what this is about, and you are not to say otherwise."

Arthur looked at him. Then he bowed his head.

Uther turned back to Merlin.

"I'm here to bring Arthur back," Merlin told them.

"You can do that?" Uther asked.

"Powerful warlocks can," Olivie told him.

"Well, why haven't you brought him back yet?"

Merlin looked at Arthur.

"Because…I've been trying, but Arthur doesn't want to."

"What are you saying?" Olivie said.

"Arthur is going through a great deal of pain," Merlin answered. "He does not want to go through any more, which is all he will find if he returns. But there will not be pain forever. I can't explain it, but Arthur is meant to end all these wars. There's a future for everyone, for Rome, for Demetia, for Caledonia, but that future depends upon Arthur. He must return, or all the darkness that is now falling upon all the lands will soon snuff out every torch, and none will be lit again."

Uther turned to Arthur. "You know of this?" he asked.

Arthur nodded.

"And yet you refuse to help? And yet you refuse to do what's right?"

"Why do I have to go back there? I already lost you, but I'm with you again. I'm with Olivie again. And soon we'll all be here."

"How do you think your mother feels?" Uther said, a red rage upon the face of his glowing form. "How do you think your mother feels knowing that you can return and yet you won't? How do you think your mother feels knowing that you can save everyone and everything, and yet you choose not to? I am gone, Arthur. I am gone. Igraine will never see me again until she joins me here, and that cannot be amidst this. Even if it was tomorrow, if that tomorrow was still a day amidst this darkness, it cannot be. But if things had somehow been lightened again, then tomorrow is tomorrow. But neither your mother, nor anybody else, deserves to perish amidst this turmoil. And you can save them, Arthur. You can save your family."

Arthur looked at him.

Merlin and Olivie looked at each other.

"I am your friend," Uther said, after a moment of silence had elapsed. "Truly, I am. But more importantly, I am your father. As your friend, I know the pain you are enduring, and more. And as a friend, I would say I support you, and that you have the choice to remain here, to let everything else burn and find the peace you've been looking for. But as your father, I must say that doing that is wrong. Yes, these people will all die, but that's not the point. Death should be at the hands of nature and time, not madmen and darkness. That's not the way of things. As your father, I must tell you that you must go back. You must save their lives. You must save your mother. If you don't, the peace you feel now is not true. If you let this darkness snuff out the light, you will spend the eternity that your spirit lives regretting, being angry. But if you do the right thing, you will have true peace."

Arthur looked at him.

"Arthur," Olivie said. "You must do what's right. You must. Return my father to the light. End the wars. End all the suffering. And don't let our deaths have been for nothing."

Arthur looked at her. "I understand what you ask of me." He looked back at his father. "I do. But I cannot do it. I failed once. You died. I died. Demetia was lost." Arthur shook his head. "If I go back, I will only create false hope. And false hope is worse than knowing your doom is near. Because when you hope, and that hope is crushed, it is a more devastating thing than anything else."

He looked at Merlin. "I'm sorry."

And then he disappeared.

Uther was looking at where he had been, as was Olivie.

"Uther, Olivie," Merlin said, "there is something I regret I must ask of you."

They both looked at him.

"Clearly, Arthur listens to you more than he does to me. I need you to convince him that he must return. The fate of the world is depending on it."

"How do you know this?" Uther asked.

Merlin looked at them.

"I can tell you," he said, "but you cannot tell Arthur. Knowing one's future, if good, usually tends to make it bad, and knowing one's future, if bad, usually tends to make it true."

"We swear not to tell him," Olivie said.

Merlin thought for a moment.

"Arthur is destined to reunite the tribes of the Isle, to accomplish what our predecessors three thousand years ago failed to do, to wield the sword of light again, and to establish true peace and stability. Without him, it cannot happen."

"What happened three thousand years ago?" Uther asked. "Rome wasn't even around."

"No, it was not. But I am not the right person to tell you what happened. Amidst Starhearth there are two souls who can tell you and Arthur. Their names are Mergus Megolin, and Raylon Fergus."

"Raylon Fergus. The first Fergus king of Caledonia?" Olivie asked.

Merlin nodded.

"And Mergus Megolin is a predecessor of yours?"

"Aye."

Uther looked at him. "We'll speak to them," he said.

"Thank you. But I'm telling you again, Arthur must return. He must. The fate of the world is depending on him."

He opened his eyes and saw Arthur before him.

"You're almost home, cousin," he said.

Merlin got down from the wagon as the column kept

walking and went up to Verovingian, atop his saddle and beyond the ring of Royal Guards.

"Verovingian," Merlin said.

His friend turned to see him.

"My prince. Shall I send for your horse?"

"No, thank you, friend. Whoever has it now most definitely needs it more than I do. I can walk."

Verovingian nodded. "How is Arthur?" he asked quietly.

"He will be well," Merlin said.

He felt he had peace again. Everything felt certain. Olivie and Uther would be able to convince Arthur to return, and he would return a healed man.

The sky was lead, and the sun's rays seemed to struggle to get through the clouds, but the horizon didn't seem as bleak anymore.

Then he remembered something.

He reached for the waterskin at his side, gleeful, and drank from it.

It tasted foul.

8

SANCTUARY

THE HOURS FELT LIKE DAYS as the sun rose higher. At midday, they heard the far-off roar of thunder and looked to see a brooding mass, black and lighting up here and there with lightning, approaching from the east.

"We will not stop," Megolin said. "We are three hours from Gilidor, and we cannot waste more time."

So, they kept marching.

And then the storm winds began to rise.

The trees creaked and cracked. Twigs snapped off from the branches, and the leaves that blanketed the ground swirled around them like bees swarming a foraging bear.

Even with his hood up, Merlin could still feel the wind pelting the back of his head.

The crack of lightning set the horses to neighing, and then the roaring thunder drowned out all other noise.

A little while later, the rains began to fall. They pinged off armor, battered the oaken wagons, turned the road to mud, and soaked Merlin and all of the rest to the bone.

The wind lashed his face with water, and Merlin had to squint to see. His cloak snapped and billowed as he fought to walk, with the mud holding back his legs.

He looked at the wagon carrying Arthur. Its wheels were sinking further in the ruts as the horses struggled to bear it forward, their hooves scratching the ground more than plodding forward.

No one ate, and for that, Merlin was grateful.

The water tasting foul after he had spoken to Uther and Olivie had just been too much for him to handle. Time was running out, and Arthur was not going to return. Merlin felt the tugging at his heart more painfully now. And though it was raining, he could feel himself sweating, and he was colder than any storm had the right to make him.

He looked at the wagon again and chanted some spell of the old speech.

At once, the wagon stopped sinking, and the horses found it easier to heave the cart forward.

At least he hadn't failed at that.

The storm slowed them, so they arrived a few hours after Megolin had said they would.

Merlin was staring at the ground when Verovingian stopped beside him. "Merlin!" he yelled over the wind and rain.

Merlin stopped and was raising his head to see him when he spotted the great star fortress rising up from the green fields. Stony and bleak, the wind howled around the points of the star that bristled with scorpions and boasted granite watchtowers with fires burning at the top that rose higher still from the battlements, lined with archers standing to attention, and a row of iron torches crackling before them, guttering from the wind.

The main gate was a giant portcullis. Its heavy iron bars looked black amidst the darkness of the storm. Two standards flanked the gate, heavy from the rain, and boasted the crest of the De Grance clan, a glowing torch amidst a field of green.

Merlin eyed the battlements as their own standard hung soaked and heavy beside Megolin.

Everyone stood still as the rains poured, the lightning cracked, and the thunder roared.

As Merlin fought to see through the darkness and the rain, he saw the iron portcullis begin to rise, but they could not hear the rattling of chains or the iron creak.

Its muddy spikes rose up from the ground and stopped twelve feet above.

Megolin trotted forward. The Royal Guards ahead of

him who had been watching trotted ahead, and then the entire column was marching toward the gate.

Only when Merlin was standing there did he actually see how monstrous the fortress was. The battlements seemed a hundred feet away, supported by layer upon layer of great granite blocks held secure by mortar, with the torches that lined the crenelations appearing as small fireflies from where he stood.

The arch of the portcullis seemed to be guarded by a wall of water that ended at the ground where a great muddy puddle had formed.

Merlin saw his father, Igraine, and the Royal Guards go through, and then he couldn't see beyond the shield of rain.

Merlin and Verovingian followed.

They walked through the curtain of water to find some respite from the rains once they stood beneath the portcullis. Verovingian's horse whickered, its breath misting before its nose. Merlin looked behind and saw that the wagon carrying Arthur was moving through the first curtain of water.

Another shield awaited at the end of the archway, three granite blocks away, and beyond that, more rain that turned the ground a muddy, slippery landscape.

When they walked out of the archway, they found a second wall with another gate and walked through to find Megolin and Igraine awaiting them at the gate of the bailey that separated the receiving yard from the rest of the city.

Verovingian swung down from his horse, and holding it with the reins, walked with Merlin to the gate as the rest of their column filed through the main one.

A few wooden buildings crowded the other end of the yard.

They were the barracks, Merlin surmised.

When they reached the bailey, a lad ran up to walk Verovingian's horse away.

Standing by the gate, with a granite arch shielding them from the rain, Merlin lowered his hood as water flowed off his hair and face and puddled around his shoes.

"Your Grace," Verovingian said, bowing his head. "Lady Igraine."

"Father. Aunt," Merlin greeted them.

The turned as the wagon carrying Arthur stopped just by the raised gate.

Then they turned and walked through. The rains were no less merciful there, but there were more buildings here. The muddy, puddled road was lined with oaken taverns and shops. The rain flowed off the slate roofs and poured onto the street a few yards away from the doors of the shops.

Signs hung from the sides of the buildings, swinging from the wind, though the squeak of the iron bars that anchored them to the building was lost amidst the howling wind and thunderous rains.

Merlin and Verovingian followed the rest of the royal family and the Royal Guards towards the end of the street.

Merlin had been here before. The last time, High General Meerbark had met them at the main gate and told them of the changes he'd made to the city. But now, with the dark tidings that were being received from all corners of the Isle, and with rains almost as heavy as their sorrow, no one was particularly keen about sightseeing or boasting of the fortress.

There was another wall at the end of the street. From here, Merlin saw it wrapping around the second ring of the city. It too was crowned with merlons and torches, and there were huts along the battlements for garrison soldiers to seek shelter and rest, unlike the first wall, and there weren't as many soldiers watching from this one.

The portcullis began to rise as they approached. By the time they got there, it was already high enough for all of them to walk through to the third ring.

Gilidor was broken up into four rings, as Merlin had learned the first time he had seen the city with his father. The first was occupied by half the garrison. The second and third were where the townsfolk lived, and the fourth was where the keep and the rest of the ten-thousand strong garrison was.

Land's End was a maritime nation. Three of its borders were with the sea, one with the Narrow Sea, the western one with the Great Ocean, and the northern one with the Emerald Sea. There were some threats beyond that, but the Rodwinians had long since lost their maritime supremacy. All of Land's End's major threats were from the rest of the land.

Gilidor, though it was at the border with Demetia, was meant to guard Land's End from more northern threats. A series of forts with Gilidor at the center formed the center of Land's End's defense, protecting what little land Land's End owned that bordered Rodwin to the Narrow Sea.

Merlin hoped it would be enough to hold back the tidal wave that was drowning all the Isle with fire.

Beyond the gate to the second ring, a host of guards greeted them.

The rain pelted their iron scale armor as they stood there, their spears towering above them.

Standing before them was their general, the castellan of Gilidor. Meerbark's pauldrons bore the torch of the De Grance clan, as did his cuirasse. His vambraces were polished steel, and the elbows of his hauberk could be seen between them and his pauldrons. His knees boasted leather caps, and his shoes were laced sandals.

The helm he held at his side was an iron halfhelm with an iron spike jutting up.

Megolin approached him, the army of cloaks snapping and swirling.

"Your Grace," Meerbark shouted, bowing his head. "We all offer you our condolences for the loss of Demetia! Our prayers go to those who were left behind."

"Thank you," Megolin yelled. "Alas, I had hoped we'd meet again amidst better conditions. But today, my people and I arrive at Gilidor as refugees. We request shelter till the storm moves on, and then I'm leaving for the capital. And, I must tell you, we have two bodies with us."

Meerbark nodded and turned to his men. "Split!" he yelled.

The formation of fifty guards broke into two, and Megolin walked between, followed by Igraine, Merlin, Verovingian, and the cart bearing Arthur.

Merlin saw Verovingian eyeing the cart as it rattled past, heading towards the keep.

9

DRAGON
AT THE CAPITAL IN LAND'S END

T HE STORM HAD LASHED THE ground for two days. Sheets of ice had formed on the buildings and the gates and even the fields. But the clouds had cleared, and the sun had returned.

Within hours of the storm's end, the sun's rays had melted away the ice, and the cold was beginning to lighten.

One by one, people began reemerging from their homes, and the city returned to life.

But Guinevere hadn't needed for the cold to lift.

Once the rains stopped, she snuck out of the keep and ran off to the oak grove.

Autumn had rid the branches of most of their leaves,

and the rains had turned the grove into a damp, heavy, mushy world.

But the nineteen year old Guinevere did not find herself sinking. With a simple spell, she walked across the ground as light as air.

The ancient barks were carved with old faces.

Who had actually carved them was still a mystery to the warlocks, and to even the wisest warlocks of earlier times. But everyone knew they were carved by good souls, and the belief spun around them was that they were the faces of ancient powers beyond the average fellow's ken, and that only the wisest could directly communicate with them.

Guinevere approached one of the trees.

Its carved eyelids were shut, and the branch that formed its nose was gnarled. The slash that was its lips was a mean line, and all its face was wrinkled with a thousand fissures that ran across the gnarly bark.

"Speak to me, for I am here to know," she said to the face.

At once, the eyelids flicked open, revealing golden orbs where the black of a person's eyes were.

The rest of the bark moved with its face as it frowned.

"Why do you wake the sleeping?" it asked with a voice old and calm.

"I'm here to learn," she said. "I may be talented, but my magic isn't as powerful as it should be yet."

The ancient face looked at her. "Practice," it croaked. "Practice. And don't wake the sleeping."

The tree closed its eyes again, and then it was just a carving.

Guinevere shook her head and turned around.

She raised her hand, and a blue orb launched from it. Crackling and trailing blue, it sailed between the trees and struck the canopy. A few leaves and twigs snapped off, but nothing more.

Then she conjured another one with each of her palms and held them together.

The great blue orb grew as she supplied more energy through her arms, and then she let it fly towards the heavens.

The thing sped past the canopy and rose up high above the city. For a long time, she watched as it flew upward, so bright that she could still see it from where she stood.

She was sure that if anyone looked up, they'd see it, too.

But then, after a while, the orb lost its energy, disintegrated till it seemed a pebble, and was gone.

Guinevere looked again at the trees around her, all carved with sleeping faces.

She closed her eyes and imagined a little beast that glowed blue. Its tail was bristling with thorns, and its wings and head were scaled. Its teeth were as sharp as a shark's, and its eyes were ice blue.

She opened her eyes, and it was there, walking across the ground, blue tendrils rising from it.

It looked at her, and then breathed a lance of blue flame that cut through the air, illuminating the surroundings with blue fire. When the flame disappeared, she saw that smoke was rising from its nostrils.

It ran forward, kicking up the leaves, and then launched from the ground.

Guinevere laughed as it fluttered around, struggling to stay airborne, and then crashed back to the ground.

Poor thing. She swiped her hand, and the dragon dispersed into blue dots of light that floated away.

Perhaps she would do better with creatures she knew more about. She slipped away from the most ancient oaks, conjuring rabbits here, squirrels there, and cats and dogs amongst them. They all loped after her, which made her laugh.

"Lady Guinevere!" A baritone voice sounded through the trees.

At once, the glowing forms began to disperse, and Guinevere ran to a tree and looked around.

"Lady Guinevere!" The voice yelled again. "Your lord parents told you not to wander around with your magic!"

Lord's Guards. Guinevere squinted and saw a group of them walking through the trees, their scale armor reflecting the light of the sun.

Didn't they realize she needed to practice? How could she help in this oncoming war if she barely understood her magic? "I am practicing!" she said. "In the oaken grove, as I have promised to do."

"It is not safe for you here alone," the captain said. "Come out."

"I must be here."

The guards dashed toward her, herding her back toward the keep, and she sighed. Then, she chanted a spell, and they all disappeared.

"What is this?" One of them shouted, and then she heard the sound of crashing armor as two of them collided with each other.

She laughed and ran past them as they struggled to find their footing.

"Guinevere, release us from this at once!" The captain bellowed. He sounded closer than he had been, though. The others blocked her path back to the oak grove, and they were coming at her quickly. She ran.

As she reached the edge of the oak grove, she raised the invisibility spell. She didn't want people running into them in the city.

"Guinevere!"

She darted out of the oak grove and ran along a street where stall owners had set up their shops.

A cart that had been overturned when she passed this way before was already back up, though there were still a few apples and barrels of spice and other fruits on the ground.

She harnessed the energy of the universe to return the shopkeeper's goods to their proper places as she ran past.

"Lady Guinevere!" The captain yelled. "Stop this madness at once!"

Stop what madness? Her magic? She couldn't even if she wanted to. Wouldn't they rather she learned how to control it? Guinevere kept running, tapping into the energy of the universe again to topple an empty wagon before the guards.

"Gods!" One of them swore as he stopped before he could collide with it.

She cast a spell of invisibility upon them once more and heard them shout and collide with each other as she ran off toward the Green Keep.

Its stone facade rose high from the center of the city, and she could see the guards walking the parapets.

The streets here were still crowded with stalls and customers, and wagons rattled here and there. A cacophony of voices could be heard from all the blocks of the city, and Guinevere found she did not even need the guards to be invisible and falling over themselves for her to lose them.

So, she lifted the invisibility once more, but kept running.

Within moments, she was running through the Torch Gate, and then she saw her parents standing at the doors of the Green Keep.

The captain and his guards thundered through a moment later, tired and cursing.

"Guinevere!" her father yelled. "You have been told not to disturb the people with your magic! And you have been told not to cast your spells upon anyone else!"

"It was not anything harmful," Guinevere said. "And I must know how to control my powers."

"Perhaps," her father said, sharply, "but you are nevertheless a disturbance to the people. So, stop bothering them."

"Your lord father is right," her mother told her. "You are powerful, but that does not mean you can practice those powers anywhere. You have chosen the oaken grove. Practice your powers there. And don't make anyone invisible again. I can imagine it is quite disturbing."

"I was trying to practice in the oaken grove, but they came and chased me out," Guinevere said.

Her father huffed and turned back to the doors of the keep. "It is not safe in the oaken grove today."

Her mother followed.

Guinevere paused, thinking through whether to follow or return to the grove.

The captain of the guard approached and grabbed her arm as if to drag her in by force.

Guinevere launched a wave of energy that pushed him and his men away.

They staggered backward, their armor clattering as it struck the stone wall.

She hurried up the steps to get into the keep before the doors closed.

Her mother glared at her.

"You said no invisibility," she said, "and that was not a spell."

Her father looked as if he was about to say something, but then he turned and walked off.

Her mother shook her head. "Little Guinevere," she said, "there is still much that you do not know."

And then she turned and left her, too.

The torches along the hall crackled.

Guinevere scowled after her parents. She hadn't been "Little Guinevere" in a long time.

However, she agreed there was much she didn't know.

That was exactly why she needed to practice.

10

GILIDOR
AT GILIDOR IN LAND'S END

THE STORM WAS LIGHTENING, BUT the last rains were still falling. It pattered off the slate roofs and stone blocks of the fortress city but was light enough that the stalls had returned, and people were going about their normal lives.

Word of the Demetians' arrival at Gilidor was already known by all the people of the city, and a messenger had already been sent to the capital. Megolin and his family had been given the royal chambers at the top of the keep, but Merlin had refused to rest until Arthur had returned.

And now they were all seated before High General Meerbark's table. The solar was comfortably warmed by

125

a dozen candles that burned along the walls and the great hearth that crackled behind the table, which was cluttered with maps and papers and books.

Merlin, Igraine, Megolin, and Clyde were seated across from Meerbark as he looked at the map that showed the coastline of the Isle and the cities and towns from the Narrow Sea to halfway through the neutral land, occupied by Rodwin and Astavon and the other major tribes of Britannia.

Merlin knew that Meerbark was looking at Demetia and the distance between it and Gilidor.

"First, I sincerely apologize for the losses you have all endured. But I'm afraid there is no time for reminiscence right now. Can you tell me what happened?"

"It started before the last black moon," Megolin said. "The Romans landed at Inver Ridge. Their leaders were the exiled Pendragon clan, if I speak truly. Uther Pendragon was the rightful heir to the imperial throne of Rome, and his son was Arthur. Uther was my sister's husband and Arthur her son. After they landed, Arthur went to Demetia, looking for my son, Merlin. We met him and afterward he headed back north to Inver Ridge.

"By that point, a stranger had joined them. I am told that that man claimed to be Uther's first son, and that the elder Pendragon named him his heir. His relationship with Arthur splintered at that point.

"Soon after that, the Highlanders sent a party to meet the Romans. The Princess Olivie and General Magi Ro

Hul, who is now either dead or a prisoner of the Huns, arrived at Inver Ridge. Arthur proved his peaceful behavior towards them, when King Fergus had already been slighted that he had treated with us. But the relation was good, and Arthur requested permission to marry his daughter.

"King Fergus consented, and they were scheduled to wed, but then some kind of deal was struck with Arthur's now estranged father who had named this outsider, who now calls himself Gallagher Pendragon, heir. It's clear now, though, that he works for the enemy. He impressed Fergus by defeating a Hun attack at Dornoch, and since he is the heir to the Roman Empire, Fergus decided to betroth him to Olivie and to arrest Arthur. Arthur escaped, and Olivie refused to marry the barbarian. For that, she was imprisoned. Arthur and Merlin went to rescue her, but she was killed. And then the war started. Fergus ordered Gallagher and Magi Ro Hul to attack Demetia, burn our cities, find Arthur, and end his life. But Magi Ro Hul stayed true to Arthur and to us, and helped us defend Demetia from the Huns' prisoners he had captured at Dornoch.

"After this, Arthur tried to gain the alliance of the other lordships, but they all refused, and he and Uther, who had returned to his senses, fell trying to defend Demetia one last time. We had to retreat when an army of almost a hundred thousand, many of whom had sailed from the Continent just recently, set Demetia to burning."

He paused.

"It took three days for us to get here. There are eight

thousand of us, and three hundred soldiers. We were ambushed by the Huns when we were still thirty miles or so from here, but we managed to defeat them with minimal losses. Along the way, we lost a hundred because of their wounds."

He looked at Meerbark.

"We were a wounded party. Most of us weren't soldiers. And it took us three days to get here. The Huns could be at your doorstep at any moment if you aren't prepared. And I fear the only reason they're not here yet is because they're preparing for a grand attack. They will not test your defenses. They will not ambush or commit sudden attacks. They will charge with force of a hundred thousand soldiers, and they will not be easily defeated."

Meerbark eyed him, his whitening brows frowning. "Gilidor is garrisoned by ten thousand men. The battlements are armed with countless more scorpions, and there is an army of trebuchets ready to be deployed. And then there is the line of lesser forts. Can that hold them?"

Megolin looked at him. "I regret to say that you ought not to trust all this will. They are a vile people, General, capable of all means of war. They build weapons well for how stupid they are. And stupid is difficult to defeat, unless you can form a strategy. But Land's End only has, even if you recruit all who can be recruited, only a hundred thousand soldiers. The Huns have more who have known battle all their life. And more are arriving from the Continent every day."

Meerbark thought for a while as the Megolins eyed him.

The recounting of all that had happened had cloaked the room with a solemn air, and Igraine found it difficult to believe that all this had happened across just two months. The escape from Rome seemed a lifetime ago, when her husband and son were still alive, when her family was still together. It had been when Bulanid Mehmet did not exist, and when Britannia had been a sanctuary.

"I will send word to Lord De Grance," Meerbark said. "Troops from our other garrisons can be posted here. The people will be ready to evacuate within a moment's notice. As for your travel to the capital, carriages will be supplied you and your guards. You will arrive a day and a half after you leave, unless you take the rest of your people with you."

"Very good," Megolin said.

"Who is Arthur?" Meerbark asked Merlin. "The men say he was glowing blue. I may be a warrior, and I may be a Land's Ender, but I know of the magic of Demetia. That was a spell of containment."

Merlin looked at him. "Arthur is the chosen one," he said, solemnly. "He is supposed to unite the Isle and end our civil wars for all time. His death is not supposed to be, and I can revive him."

Meerbark eyed him.

"My condolences, Lady Igraine, and I apologize, but the world has moved on from that. There's never going to be a chosen, and the Isle is never going to unite again. We tried once, and our king ruined everything. Lords would sooner spill their own blood than suffer the craziness of another national king. Still, I am sure Arthur was a good man. If you can revive him, he can help us."

"More than you know," Merlin said. He rose. "Forgive me," he said, then turned to leave.

"My son is not the chosen one because of a prophecy," Igraine said when Merlin was gone. "He is the chosen one because of who he is. Have some faith, general, and I promise you it will help everyone."

She and Megolin rose. "Farewell, General." She turned and left, leaving Megolin and the Land's Ender.

"We are statesman and military commanders, you and I," Megolin said. "But Merlin and Igraine, and even Lord De Grance's daughter, they are of a different world. And they see things we cannot. I was convinced of who Arthur is a long time ago. And I know that he is no false hope."

Meerbark looked at him frankly. "I hope you are right, Your Grace. Because if he is the chosen one, he is the only thing that can save the Isle."

11

A FATHER

ARTHUR HAD BEEN PLACED ATOP a stone slab, his hands clasping his sword, his armor cleaned and polished. Lord Meerbark had seen him to pay his respects, as he had been King Megolin's nephew, and now the room was quiet.

Candles burned by the window and torches crackled by the door. Outside the window, a light drizzle was falling, the last of this autumn storm. The sky was lead, and the city seemed colorless, but the people were more alive than the weather was. The marketplace was alive with chatter, and the streets were crowded with carriages and people.

Merlin looked at Arthur.

131

He closed his eyes and appeared a moment later amidst the stars of Starhearth. "Uther!" Merlin yelled.

He appeared at once.

"What is it?" he asked.

"We have arrived at Gilidor, the fortress city at the border with Land's End. Land's End is the only place that the fighting hasn't reached yet. How is Arthur?"

"Arthur refuses to speak to me," he said. "He's running. Olivie and I have contacted the elder Fergus and Megolin. They have said they're also trying to look for him, but Arthur keeps running. He wants no part of this. Is Igraine all right?"

Merlin nodded. "What were they like? Fergus and Mergus? I've never met them."

"They are wise," he said. "And they know a great deal more than we do. They say Arthur is the chosen one as well."

Merlin felt relief, relief that he was right, because now he knew that everything would be fine.

"Don't worry," Uther told him. "Arthur will return. He is stronger than he knows. He will get out of his pain, and he will be the just and wise king that all the world needs. He will heal not just Britannia, but Rome as well. I know it. But things will get dark before the light shines. You will have to fight."

"We know," Merlin said. "But how? The north is still allied with the Huns. Magi Ro Hul and his army have either been slain or imprisoned. The other kingdoms are not powerful enough to fight the enemy themselves, and multiple kingdoms have already fallen."

"You must not think about numbers. Just keep fighting, and do not lose hope. Hope will allow even the last candle to stay alight. And when the time is right, Arthur will save us all."

Merlin found himself panicking but breathed and calmed himself before he broke down. Because if he did now, he knew he would not be able to rebuild himself.

"Goodbye, Uther," he said.

And then he returned to Gilidor.

He left the chamber and hurried to the steps. His legs felt as weak as dough, and he could feel his head growing light.

He rushed to the third level where one of the keep's postern gates were.

"Drop it," he said to the two guards who flanked the oaken drawbridge.

One of them turned and turned the wheel to lower the drawbridge.

The gust of icy wind that struck Merlin's face seemed to help as the drawbridge landed.

Merlin walked out at once.

The light rain was hitting his face and pattering off the stone battlements. His hair and cloak snapped and billowed, and Merlin held the stone for support as he fought to regain his mind and arrest his fear.

His head was still light, and he found it difficult to breathe, but he just closed his eyes and cleared his head.

When he opened them, he diverted his focus to the city. Beyond the section of the wall of the keep a few yards away, the city's rings were alive with people, and Merlin remembered just how much of a city Gilidor was. Even from here, where he could only see a few blocks out, the city was ten times what Demetia was.

But Merlin had never cared about that, nor had his people. Land's End grew rich from trade and maritime business. Demetia got a portion of that profit, but Demetians had never seen the importance of building grand cities. Grand cities were not the way of warlocks and the wise. So that profit was saved. Demetia was a peaceful nation, but the world had not yet moved away from war. And Demetia could not be defenseless, so a great deal of their coin went towards making sure their armies were ready for a fight, but as all the kings of Demetia had sworn for thousands of years, they would never start a war.

The thoughts about his people and his nation seemed to calm him.

The rain didn't feel like arrows anymore, and Merlin found that he no longer needed the support of the merlon.

But the dreadful feeling still hung over him.

He kept hearing Uther's words.

"…things will get dark before the light shines…"

Merlin walked back across the drawbridge.

He heard the links rattling and the drawbridge creaking as it closed once more.

C.J. BROWN

12

ANCIENT HISTORY

MERLIN STILL HADN'T BEEN ABLE to drink. He could feel he was weakening. With every hour, he felt himself growing parched, but the water was too foul.

Dawn had arrived, and with it, the last of the storm's drizzles were falling.

A lead sky, dark and gloomy, hung above the fortress like a cloak that shielded the ground from the sun. A layer of fog blanketed the city's streets, and the air was damp and heavy as the light rain fell.

Merlin found himself having to have to fight to breathe as his horse walked across the yard.

Beside him, Megolin sat atop his destrier, and to his left

was Igraine. They were surrounded by Royal Guards who moved out of the gate as they approached the portcullis.

Merlin tried to look through the fog that threatened to remain for hours more.

Meerbark was there and had summoned all his guards and elite soldiers to accompany their king's departure. But the fog bank was so heavy that Merlin couldn't see more than a few of the soldiers.

Silently, Merlin and the rest of his family and the carriage carrying Arthur and Uther left the city.

The great stones that rose high around them were themselves obscured by the mist which hid the battlements that loomed high above.

Somehow, everything about the scene made Merlin feel uneasy.

But he told himself he was being crazy.

They emerged from the fog bank minutes later to look upon a green field, dotted by autumn trees. They could see the lordsroad now. It was a great rutted path that went on towards the capital of Land's End.

Flanked by thistles and hedges and plants, the road was not littered with wagons and weapons and ash like the streets of Demetia had been.

Merlin felt sadness when he saw how the fighting had not yet turned this green field to a wasteland. There were farms nearby, Merlin knew, that had not yet been torched. And Merlin feared that they would be soon.

He turned and saw the great towers of Gilidor rising

out of the fog, and, though he hoped to calm his nerves, only felt doubt about whether this great fortress would be able to stay the enemy that had already stolen as much as it had.

They traveled all day, dined as they went, and didn't stop for anything but to water their horses.

When night fell, they could see the lights from homes miles away.

The pine and oak trees that dotted the fields were still partly green, though most of their leaves had fallen and the ground around them was blanketed with yellow. Merlin and his family sought shelter beside two oak trees that kept back the worst of the wind.

He placed his weapon by one of them and leaned beside it.

His horse whickered as the carriage drivers tethered their horses to the tree and as the servants set up the king's pavilion.

Two who had traveled with them from Gilidor were hunters of Land's End. As Merlin rested by the tree, they walked off with bows and quivers to find some game for supper.

Merlin remembered the first time he had traveled by horse. He had had saddle sores after just practicing. After a while, he was able to travel for a day without feeling more than a cramp. But this time, he could feel his legs were painful and felt welts across them. His back ached and Merlin could feel tears as the blood returned to it.

So, he remained silent, containing his misery.

His waterskin was beside him and he drank, not caring about the foul taste anymore.

The water tasted bitter and swampy, and he had to spit the rest out. That just made him feel worse. He was still destined for failure, his head felt as heavy as a hammer, and the pressure from dehydration made him feel like it was about to burst.

He threw the waterskin away and leaned back.

Nearby, the page was starting a fire outside Megolin's tent. Smoke rose from the hearth as embers hovered around it, heating the iron pot that hung above.

"Merlin," Megolin said. "Won't you join us?"

Clyde and Igraine were already seated by the fire, along with the carriage drivers and the two other servants.

Night had already fallen, and the sky was a dark blue with an orange hue where the sun had already disappeared.

The clouds were clearing, and a sky of stars was shining.

Peaceful, but for the army of Huns that lurked just miles away and war that had already turned all the lands outside Land's End to a battlefield.

Merlin rose, struggling to fight the cramp his back was protesting with. As he stood, the embroidery of his cloak glowed a light purple, reflecting the anger he felt amidst his calm.

He walked over to the campfire.

The iron pot was empty.

"Waiting for the hunters to return, Your Grace," the page said.

Merlin just nodded as the fire crackled.

They sat silently as they waited for the hunters to return.

They did, an hour later, each carrying a few rabbits.

They dropped them by the page.

"Best we could find," one of them said.

"It'll do," he answered and then started removing the fur and skin as one of the other servants prepared the soup.

But Merlin did not see any of that. He thanked Gaea for the fire, and for the safety that could still be found amidst Land's End. As the stew boiled above the fire, Merlin's mind drifted to Arthur and how to get him to return.

A revival was not only dependent upon the ability of the sorcerer. It was also greatly dependent upon the will of the subject. If the subject refused to return, only the most powerful spells could revive them, and their souls would be dark when they awoke. It would only make things worse for that person and those who missed him.

Merlin thought about how Mergus and Fergus were going to speak to him. They would tell him about the history of the Isle, Merlin knew, and how things needed to be healed and Britannia must be united. They would tell him about Excalibur, the blessed, spell-forged blade of the king who would unite the lords and peoples.

But Merlin knew Arthur was not the kind of person who cared about being a chosen one. And if what Merlin had told him about how the light was growing dark didn't change his mind, Merlin feared nothing would.

Merlin shook his head. He could not let himself fall to despair. Hope, as Merlin had learned his predecessors said during the War of the Light, was what would light the way, was what would ensure that their cause triumphed no matter what.

As long as one had hope, one could trust the cosmos would tend towards them. Lose hope, and that was the end of things.

A few minutes later, Lukan was scooping out the rabbit stew and serving them.

Merlin looked at the stew. There were carrots and onions and rabbit floating around. Merlin was famished, and he started eating.

Thankfully, the food was not foul, and Merlin found some his clarity returning.

When his bowl was empty, he placed it by the fire.

Because of the food, he no longer felt weak, and because it did not taste foul, he felt something of happiness again, despite everything that had happened.

He looked at the waterskin at his side.

A part of him feared that failure was still his destiny, so he did not reach for it.

Supper had been a silent matter, and once everyone had cleared their bowls, the pot was empty.

The page removed it from the fire and stoked the logs. Merlin rose.

"Forgive me, Father, Aunt, but I must take my leave." Megolin nodded.

Merlin rose and walked away from the fire.

All the horses had been tethered to the same tree and were chewing the greenery they'd found.

Merlin walked past and to the carriage where Arthur was.

Standing before the wagon, Merlin closed his eyes and went to Starhearth.

"King Mergus!" He yelled.

The ancient king and warlock appeared before him.

His purple robes glowed blue, and his crown was a golden ring.

He smiled at Merlin.

"King Mergus," Merlin bowed his head.

"We are family, child. To you, I am Grandfather Mergus."

Merlin looked at him.

This was the first time he had ever met him. The spirit who stood before him had lived three thousand years ago, fought battles long forgotten, and seen a time many called the golden age, and the dark age of Britannia.

"There is much we have to talk about," Mergus said.

"But there are other things of greater importance that must be discussed."

"Yes. How is Arthur?"

"We have not spoken to him yet."

Merlin stared at him. "Why?"

"Telling one he is chosen for something never turns out well." Mergus' face was grim.

"I thought so, but what makes you say that? If Arthur knew who he was, how important he is, he would return. Not telling him that hasn't helped."

"Trust me, Merlin. He cannot know he is the chosen one."

"How else can you get him to understand?"

Mergus looked at him. "He will have to think it's not supposed to be him, but that he's the only around who can."

"Why?"

Mergus eyed him. "Your father never told you?"

"No."

Mergus considered for a moment. "Three thousand years ago," he said, "Britannia was at war. King Jon of Rodwin had declared himself King of the Isle and set out from his castle to accept the fealty of the kings. At the time, his people were the best warriors, and their fleet was the greatest the Isle had ever seen."

—

As Mergus spoke, a vision unfolded before Merlin.

A great crowd of people had gathered before the Grand Palace.

Dizzying marble pillars rose up high, supporting a gilded roof with an iron spike that rose higher still.

The surrounding buildings were almost as rich. Each door was crested with the iron spike of the House of Hyron, each porch littered with fresh rushes, and each column white marble.

The balconies were all manned by the lord's guards, though now their attire was golden plate and scale armor. Their cloaks were white, and their helms boasted iron spikes.

Watching from their nests, they kept a lookout for possible threats amidst the crowd that had gathered to hear their king's words.

The entire city, essentially, was now standing before the marble steps to the palace.

They cheered as kites sailed the sky, singers sang, and musicians played.

No one knew why the king had called for such a meeting, but one never said no to the chance to meet their leader.

A herald ascended the steps and stood before the doors to the palace.

The musicians stopped and silence settled on the palace grounds.

"Royal subjects! Esteemed nobles! You have all been

gathered here for a declaration that King Jon wishes to make! Here he is, now."

The herald moved aside, and the doors opened to reveal the king.

His golden crown shone as he emerged from the palace, his golden cloak trailing behind as his retinue of guards walked beside him.

He wore golden armor, rings, and a diamond necklace, and his greatsword shone with rubies and gemstones.

His eyes were a cold blue, but he always looked upon his people with care.

"My friends!" He shouted. "Today is an auspicious day! This great kingdom, the heart of maritime trade and the owners of the greatest fleet the world has ever seen, richer than all the others, wiser than all the others, is destined for greatness!" The people cheered, and then he raised his hand for silence.

"This kingdom is great, but is this it? Is this enough? Is a few ships and a few cities really all that there is? Or is there more? More that ought to be ours? For thousands of years, the kingdoms of the Isle have been allies and enemies. And no one but us have been able to rise thanks to these wars. And now we are capable of defeating any attack. No army has reached the gates of this city for a thousand years. Other kingdoms are forming alliances with us. The Isle is rallying to our side because we are the heart of the Isle. We are the greatest power. But there are still those who remain aloof. There are still those who seek power themselves, and those who wish to remain distant. That cannot be allowed. A nation is about unity. And if there is a group of people who are not with us, they are our enemies. So, I have decided that all those loyal to me and those who will swear allegiance, will live as subjects of a mighty empire. Crops will never suffer again. Farmers will never worry about supper. Soldiers won't have to always be posted somewhere. Wars can stop. Unity can be. But those who refuse to join me will suffer fire and steel. I am a just king. The just will benefit, and the unworthy will fall."

A great cheer erupted, and Jon smiled.

"I hereby declare this kingdom an empire, the rightful seat of the Isle, and its people, the rightful owners of the Isle. All our armies and all our ships will deploy. Emissaries will be sent to the nations who have not yet sworn allegiance, and those who have will ready their soldiers for war. A new age is upon us. An age of unity, an age of peace, and the age of emperors!"

C.J. BROWN

13

FROM BEYOND
In Starhearth

"**A**RTHUR," FERGUS SAID.

Arthur turned to see him. "Who are you?"

"A friend," he said. "I am Raylon Fergus, the first of my clan to be king of the Highlands."

Arthur looked at him.

"You're the first King Fergus?"

"Aye. Before me there was one named Ergar. He was a wise fellow, kind and just. He was the greatest king the North ever saw."

His voice was sad, Arthur noted. "What happened to him?"

"He died, trying to attain something none of us can."

"What?"

"Power the gods do not mean for us to wield."

Arthur looked at him.

"Why are you talking to me?"

Fergus eyed him.

"Your father met with me and the ancient King Mergus of Demetia."

"My father?"

"Aye. A good man, he is. And weary for you. "

"You're here to convince to go back, aren't you?"

"No. I'm here to tell you the truth."

"What truth?"

"The truth of the Isle."

Arthur didn't say anything.

"Three thousand years ago," Fergus said, "King Jon of the greatest maritime realm the Isle had ever seen, with a fleet of a thousand ships and an army of fifty thousand, decided it was time for his people, for himself, to ascend to a greater tier of government. Jon believed it was time for the isle to unite. But his dream was not as great as you might think. He cared not for the unity or the peace of the Isle. He cared only about his own power. As sole ruler of Britannia, he would have been the most powerful man who ever lived. Britannia was once greater than Rome ever was. Our fields yielded crops enough that no town would ever starve. There were enough trees to build a thousand cities, and enough gold to enrich one for lifetimes.

"Of course, unity was something that the Isle wished

for, but unity could not be acquired at the hands of Jon. His people saw him as a friend, and those who allied with him were greedy, or trying to save their own people. But the north recognized the evil of that man before the war even started. But he had never done anything wrong, so we could not accuse him.

"When King Jon declared himself emperor and rallied his allies, I was General of Caledonia. The Highlands were defended by fifty thousand soldiers, but Jon had a hundred, thanks to his allies.

"The war arrived at Pittentrail three months after King Jon declared himself emperor. A hundred thousand soldiers besieged Pittentrail. After a week of fighting, King Ergar ordered me to prepare the city to flee, while he went north to the frozen wastelands. Emissaries from even Jon's court, from Demetia, and from a number of the kingdoms that had sworn allegiance to Jon, went with him, even the castellan of Jon's capital, who had realized his king had lost his way. By this point, Prince Mergus' father had decided to join the north, and was sending his son to Pittentrail with ten thousand men to help.

"Ergar returned with the spell-forged weapon, Excalibur. The weapon cannot be wielded by anyone not considered worthy by the Isle."

Arthur was listening, and all his troubles seemed to have disappeared.

"The blade shone, Arthur, like a torch. And with it, King Ergar returned to Pittentrail and attacked the host of soldiers encamped outside his gates. But fortune did not yet mean for this moment to be when the unjust Emperor Jon would fall and when freedom would prevail. King Ergar was slain, cut down by Jon himself. I led our people secretly out of the city, and met up with Prince Mergyle, who was also retreating from the battlefield."

"And then you ascended the throne?"

"Not yet," Fergus said. "But I think that's enough for one day."

Arthur thought for a moment. "What does this have to do with me?"

Fergus looked at him. "You will know," he said. "I cannot tell you. That will only make things worse."

"So, I still have a future?"

"Aye."

Arthur shook his head. "How could I have a future? I'm here. And when I was alive, I failed."

"What we do, alive or not, does affect those who are still alive. Trust me, Arthur, there is much you do not yet know. Now, pray forgive me. I must take my leave."

Arthur didn't say anything as Fergus disappeared and left him standing there.

Merlin reappeared a moment later.

"We were both told the same thing," he said.

Arthur looked at him.

"What does it mean?"

"It's about the future of the Isle."

14

DEFENSE OF LAND'S END
On the Road to the Capital of Land's End

D AWN ARRIVED WITH A SKY that threatened rain, but the storm still looked several hours away, so they would be able to get to the capital before the worst of the rains fell."

They had no time to waste, so Megolin agreed, and so now they were cantering west, to the sound of leather traces snapping on the horses pulling the carriage.

Merlin was starting to feel better since Arthur's demeanor was now changing.

At midday, when they stopped to water the horses, Merlin drank some water again. The foul taste was there, albeit less. That was enough.

They saddled up again, and by afternoon, a light

drizzle began to fall. With it, the winds broke branches and twigs from the trees and kicked up the autumn leaves that blanketed the ground.

Merlin's cloak snapped and swirled as the wind howled.

There was a town nearby with about a hundred shops and houses and a few watchtowers. Merlin thought they might stop here, but the page said that they could still get to Trevena. If they tried to wait out the storm, they would only be able to leave three days hence. Autumn storms were never a friend to the rushed traveler. So Megolin decided they go on, and Merlin cantered past the town with a heavy heart. But he knew what had to be done and realized that that town too would be torched if Arthur did not return and if the Isle did not defeat the Huns.

As nightfall approached, the sky grew darker and the rains heavier. Even the fields turned a dull lead, and once the sun set, all the land was shrouded with darkness.

There were no stars to light the way, and the nearest town was just a few hundred yards away, and their torches could not help.

The rain had by now soaked Merlin to the bone and he could feel the cold beginning to weaken him.

Miserable and grieving, the Megolins and their train traveled silently, enduring the drizzle and the cold and the darkness.

"Light torches," Megolin finally ordered after sunset.

The page handed three to the other servants and lit

his own with flint and steel as the others set their torches ablaze.

Light radiated from the torches, but none of them could feel the fire. The air was too cold, and their spirits too dark.

Two hours later, they spotted the Green Keep of the capital rising tall and proud from the heart of the city. Countless watchtowers with fires keeping the darkness at bay could be seen, and so could the torches of the town outside the city gates.

The streets of the town that flanked the lordsroad was empty, they saw, as they went through. Lights could be seen through the shutters of the buildings and voices could be heard now and then, but the streets were empty where the rain had turned the roads to mud and the air frigid.

Megolin reined up a few yards from the main gate of the city.

"This is King Megolin, your liege!" the page yelled.

They heard a shout and at once the great iron portcullis began to rise.

Like Gilidor, the gate was flanked by the banners of Land's End, but the city was not a star fortress.

As Merlin and his family went through, Merlin noted the second gate and wall ten yards away.

The distance between the first and second was occupied by a moat bristling with spikes, with drawbridges here and there that connected all the outer gates to the second set.

As they approached the second gate, the first closed

with an iron clang and Merlin looked up to see a hundred helms looking at them.

A bolt of lightning struck just then, and Merlin saw their faces for a moment.

Trevena's yard was nothing like Gilidor's. Rather than a mud field with barracks, the ground was cobblestone and there were stone structures with oaken shutters. A stone bridge marked the end of the yard and connected one of the watchtowers to another stone bridge that ran to the second wall.

A few soldiers were huddled by fires with their spears beside them.

They rose at once when they saw the Megolins.

"Your Grace." They bowed.

At once, hooves clattered toward them, and Merlin looked to see a column of armed guards thundering towards them, the banner of Land's End hovering above their helms.

Cloth-of-gold cloaks trailed from their shoulders, and Merlin could see that the horses, too, wore polished armor that reflected the light of the torches.

The one leading the party reined up before Megolin and swung down from his saddle.

His men followed as he bowed.

"Your Grace," he said.

"Commander," Megolin answered.

"We got the raven two days past. We are truly sorry."

"You are most kind," Megolin said. "Is Lord De Grance awake?"

"Yes, Your Grace. We will take you to him."

The commander and his guards saddled up and wheeled their horses around.

They cantered back through the archway, and Megolin, Merlin, Igraine, and their train trotted after them.

When they went through the arch, Merlin was able to see much more of the city.

It was not as militarily significant as Gilidor, and rather more suited to civilian life.

For as far as Merlin could see from his horse, there were nothing but slate and timber roofs housing the people of the capital. The streets were brightly lit with iron lanterns that hung from oaken posts, and even at night, the city was alive.

The Street of Merchants, where traders from all the known world set up their shops to sell to the locals, and which was connected to the harbor, still sounded the din of business – buyers haggling with the sellers, sellers boasting of rich spice and godly jewels.

Merlin felt a pang of sadness at hearing city life, for he knew that all this would end if the Huns prevailed, and they would prevail if Arthur did not return as the king the mages had prophesied he would be.

Great fires were burning as chatter drifted through the air. Taverns catered to soldiers and the old, who smoked their pipes, talking of the war. Children fought with wooden swords while young men trained near the barracks. Horses snickered and trotted along. Travelers ate at shops throughout the city. More people were arriving every day from the province's furthest cities. But where the enemy was attacking at their borders with the Narrow Sea, the people of Land's End remained strong. Farms fed the defenders, and the farmers built defensive walls around their fields. Their spirit was strong. Nothing would break it.

The hooves of their horses clattered off the cobblestone road as they ascended the hill, at the top of which was perched the Green Keep.

From here, Merlin could already see it.

A curtain wall bristling with merlons and scorpions, and guards hid the first levels. There seemed to be only one gate, and the portcullis, flanked by the banners of Land's End, was shut.

Torches burned everywhere, and there seemed to be no street that was left to the darkness.

From that, Merlin drew relief. There was something about light that even helped one with the lowest feelings, whereas the dark was cold and turned even the good things sour.

As the horses clattered on, Merlin kept looking at the Keep.

Tall stone spires rose from the corners of the castle, and fires burned at the top. The Keep was dotted by postern gates and there was a network of baileys all manned by guards. There must have been at least two hundred men posted strategically as far as Merlin could see. He was sure that with the advantage they had, no Hun army could ever get through.

Within a few minutes, the horses stopped before the great iron portcullis of the Green Keep.

"Raise the gate for King Megolin!" The commander of the Lord's Guard yelled.

At once, they heard the clinking of chains and the creak of iron as the gate began to rise.

Moments later, its spikes were rising up, and then hovered above the ground.

The Lord's Guard commander trotted forward, and Merlin and the rest of them followed.

The castle yard was crowded with guards and soldiers. The training yard rang with the clash of steel, and the parapets with talk of the guards.

But a hush fell when they saw the king.

They bowed.

"Return to your duties," Megolin said.

At once, the din of the yard resumed, and Megolin turned to the commander of the Lord's Guard.

"Forgive Lord De Grance," the commander said, "but he is quite busy and regrets that he could not meet you himself."

"It's good he didn't," Megolin said. "There are far more important things to tend to right now. We must meet, though."

The great oaken doors of the keep creaked just then, and a lad ran out, wearing a leather brigantine, a hooded cloak, and woolen breeches. "Your Grace." He bowed, as the rain grew heavier.

"All right, we stop now!" Merlin heard a voice shout and then the recruits were running from the yard.

"Lord De Grance will meet you now," the lad said. "He has called a meeting of the council so that you all may deliberate."

Megolin swung down from his saddle, signaling to Merlin, Igraine, and the rest of their train to do so as well.

The commander of the Lord's Guard signaled, and at once a group of lads ran over to walk their horses away.

Merlin went to the carriage where Arthur was and told the guards to send him to a chamber.

The commander of the Lord's Guard looked at the Roman with surprise.

But he knew better than to question the royal family of his people.

Without a word, he and the Megolins stepped through the doors and out of the rain.

The air here was fresh and toasty and cast drowsiness upon Merlin.

He snapped himself out of it. This was no time for sleep.

The commander of the Lord's Guard saw them to the throne room.

Servants and guards walked past as they ascended the steps, all bowing when they saw their king.

They reached the fifth level by ascending stone steps, passing windows that looked out for miles beyond the city. Some allowed for a view of a the waves of the Great Ocean that crashed along the coast. A hundred ships, half merchant, berthed there.

Two guards stood beside the doors to Lord De Grance's court. "Your Grace," they said, bowing.

Megolin nodded as they opened the doors.

The entire court had been called to meet. Lord De Grance, dressed in gold and blue livery, sat atop his throne of stone and wood. The banners of Demetia and Land's End hung behind his seat as torches and fireplaces crackled, warming the cold stone.

As Merlin walked in, the guards shut the doors, and the Megolin clan proceeded along the aisle.

Walking past ministers, advisors, and guards, all bowing, they reached the dais where De Grance knelt, with the Lady Genie to his right, and the Lady Guinevere to hers. The latter stared at them with yellow eyes.

"Your Grace," De Grance said, "great sorrow is felt tonight for the misfortunes of our people. We regret that we could not help."

"Do not spend time regretting, Leo, for there is much to do."

Leo looked at Merlin. "The last time I saw you," he

said, you were a little lad still learning to speak. Now, you are one of the greatest warlocks the Isle has ever seen."

Merlin felt a pang of pain stab through him when he heard those words. Normally, he would have been happy, but the pain of his failures made those words hollow.

But he couldn't say that.

"I thank you," he muttered.

Megolin turned and walked over to the empty seat beside Lord De Grance.

Igraine went with him, and Merlin walked to the seat opposite from Megolin, also beside De Grance.

When Megolin sat, the rest of the room sat as well.

Merlin watched as Megolin eyed the council.

"What were you just talking about?"

"We were going over the recent events that have befallen the Isle." De Grance waved at the map. Upon the location of Demetia had been placed a square timber block. All the cities that had fallen to the Huns were marked with the same tokens. "The only places not yet occupied by the enemy are Astavon, Rodwin, and all of Land's End."

Megolin looked at the map. "How many soldiers does Land's End have?"

"Fifty thousand, but that won't be enough, not if the news is true."

Megolin thought for a moment.

"Can Gilidor hold the Huns back?"

"It and its fortifications. But only for a time. Gilidor is at a strategic point and is itself a strategic castle. The one who holds it commands the battlefield. But the Huns are not like any enemy any Briton has ever fought. They will use their persons to burst through the gates if need be, and our men do not know how to fight such barbarity. If the enemy were to gain Gilidor, there is little chance they will know how to use the fortress, but attacking them there would still be difficult."

Megolin considered, and then he looked at the rest of the council.

Then he rose.

The council and the court rose as well.

"There is something that I will tell you," Megolin shouted, "but you must first swear that you will not tell a soul outside this room."

The people eyed each other.

"Of course, Your Grace," one of the councilors said.

Megolin looked at him. "The prophecy is that the Isle would one day choose someone to unite Britannia once more and wield Excalibur. That someone has been chosen."

A wave of murmurs swept through the crowd.

"Meerbark sent word of such a person that you spoke about," De Grance said.

Megolin nodded. "His name is Arthur Pendragon, son of Uther Pendragon and Igraine Megolin, my nephew, and Prince Merlin's cousin."

"The Pendragons were the emperors of Rome for decades, till Lucius the Usurper stole the throne," Igraine said. "My husband was the rightful heir to the Empire, and rather than fight Lucius for his right, he chose to spare the provinces from civil war. Now, he is gone."

"But Arthur is not," Merlin said. "He died at the Fall of Demetia, but I have anchored his spirit. He can return."

"Why hasn't he?" De Grance asked.

Merlin looked at him.

"I am not powerful enough."

"How do you know he is the one?" De Grance asked Megolin. "Perhaps that's why he cannot return. The Isle does not bring just anyone back from Starhearth."

"He is just and noble and kind," Megolin said. "And most of all, he is not of the Rome that our generation knows. He is of a better time that has not yet happened. He is the one who tried to unite the tribes just a few days ago, before the Huns attacked Demetia with all their strength. He went to try and get the Highlander king to abandon the Huns and ally with his fellow Britons, despite the hurt he had suffered because of him. He has lost a great deal, and he has not failed the light."

The lord of Land's End thought for a moment.

"We will talk more of this later. For now, we must ready ourselves for war with the Huns until Arthur can return."

Megolin nodded.

"We will send every soldier we have to Gilidor," De Grance decided, and a few to the line of forts, but Gilidor cannot fall, or the rest of Land's End will not be able to defend itself."

As her father spoke, Guinevere could tell from his demeanor that she was more able than Merlin. There was a good chance she was. Already, her spells were greater than those of many of the warlocks she learned about.

But she wouldn't say anything. She wasn't about to be arrogant.

"About seventy thousand Huns are attacking our cities and those of the other tribes," King Megolin said. "Their numbers grow every day, for the people they defeat are enslaved and added to their ranks. King Fergus has aligned with them. It's only a matter of hours before a hundred thousand Huns are at your border. There is no hope, not even with your armies. Arthur said that we should try to unite the isle. Lord Galahad is the only one who has heeded the call. Lord Lancelot marches for the trading port not far from here. Others have refused, and we haven't been able to reach the rest."

De Grance considered what his king was saying.

"Our armies number fifty thousand. There are still another fifty thousand recruitable men. Perhaps we can raise new armies and defend our borders."

"But that will take a long time, my lord," Megolin said.

De Grance considered this.

"Then we'll close off the ports and our borders. Only people of the isle will be allowed to enter. And we will send our forces to the borders. We will not let them through."

Megolin nodded.

Within the hour, as a heavy rain lashed the streets of the capital, the order was given, and the captains of the ships already docked at the port of Trevena were grounded while a battalion of soldiers marched to guard the port. Armies streamed from the gates of the city, rain pinging off their armor as birds were sent to the cities of Land's End.

15

FAILED

A S THE RAINS OF THE AUTUMN STORM Poured outside, blurring the windows, Merlin stood by Arthur. Torches illuminated the room, but Merlin could not see the light, nor feel the fires. For Merlin, the world was still too dark.

Yes, all of Land's End's armies were marching to war, and people's spirits were strong, but none of this mattered if the one thing the mages of old had prophesied did not happen. Arthur needed to return. Arthur needed to be king, and the Isle needed to rally to him. Merlin was even sure that Fergus would end his treacherous alliance with the Huns once Arthur was alive again. But that all depended upon Merlin and Arthur's will to return. Both were failing now.

Merlin closed his eyes and returned to Starhearth.

"Arthur!" he yelled.

Arthur appeared before him, his look distant.

"Arthur...did Fergus speak with you?"

Arthur nodded.

"He told me about some war three thousand years ago and how there was a king named Ergar who ruled the North."

"He told you what happened?"

"Not everything."

"Has Mergus spoken to you?"

"Yes. He said I'm a good soul." Arthur chuckled.

"Why is that funny?"

"A good soul would not have failed his people," Arthur said. "A good soul would not have suffered as much as I have."

Merlin thought for a moment. "Arthur, you did not fail your people. You fought for your people. You died for your people."

"And now they will die too," Arthur said sharply. "There are thousands of people arriving here every day. They tell tales of the fall of cities and the enemy that darkens the world. I have spoken with many of these people, Merlin. What good was my fighting for them? What good was my death and all the pain I suffered for them?"

Merlin looked at him. He hadn't realized it, but Arthur was right. With every battle the Huns fought, hundreds were being sent to Starhearth. Merlin could not imagine what their grisly tales would be like.

He realized that Arthur was battling with a far more difficult reality than he had thought.

"Arthur, I know you're suffering. I know you're angry, and you think you have failed. Right now, you haven't. But if you refuse to return, if you deny the Isle the one thing its people need to survive, you will have."

"Why am I that person? I tried uniting the tribes. It didn't work. The North is your enemy because of me. There is someone else."

"There is no one else."

Arthur looked at him.

"I'm sorry, Merlin. I've left my fighting days behind."

He began to disappear, leaving Merlin to think and fear.

When he returned to the realm of the living, Merlin found himself panicking.

He turned and left the room.

His head was spinning and light.

He raced down the steps, almost tripping as he ran.

He reached the first level of the keep moments later and ran out the oaken doors.

The cold rain chased away his plight, but just for a moment, and then he was panicking once more.

The guards who had been standing by the door looked at him with surprise.

They ran out to see him.

"My prince, are you all right?"

Merlin looked at them.

And then the world turned black.

He awoke to see Megolin and Igraine standing beside him, but then he fell asleep again.

When his opened flicked open again, the faces of Lord De Grance and Guinevere was clearer than his father's when he had seen him.

Merlin forced himself not to drift away again.

"How long?" He croaked.

"Ten hours," De Grance said.

The fog of sleep still clouded Merlin's mind. His sight blurred now and then, and his head was heavy. His ears rang and his nose was blocked.

He heard the door open and then Megolin and Igraine stepped through.

"Merlin," Megolin said, "are you all right?"

Merlin looked at his father. "I have failed," he said.

Igraine eyed him. "What do you mean?"

"Arthur wants no part of this. Mergus has spoken with him. The ancient Fergus has as well. I have. Thousands more are showing up at Starhearth every day as the Huns burn and pillage. Arthur says he has spoken to them. He says he has failed them."

Igraine looked at him. "Merlin, Arthur is not a coward.

If he says he cannot help, there is good reason. They may not be right reasons, but they are good reasons. He has lost his father. He has lost his betrothed. He has lost friends and family, both of which he also gained, but to him, he failed them, too. You have not failed, Merlin. You cannot give up. Know his pain, know his mind as best you can. And do not lose hope."

"Perhaps I can speak to Arthur," Guinevere said.

Merlin and the rest of the room looked at her.

"Guinevere," De Grance said.

"Really, I can," she said. "At least, let me try."

Merlin eyed her and noticed there was something different about her.

He had seen that she had the yellow eyes of a warlock, but now he could not understand why she did. Her father was no warlock, and a sorcerer gained power by being the child of a sorcerer.

De Grance turned to Igraine and Megolin.

"My daughter is a powerful warlock. She has had no teacher, but she has demonstrated powers beyond what some of Britannia's most powerful could wield."

"This is not about power," Merlin argued, but there was something about Guinevere's energy that he could not comprehend.

"What's wrong? Scared I'll be more powerful than you?" Guinevere asked him.

"Guinevere!" De Grance said.

"Forgive me, my prince," Guinevere said. "Still, I can try."

"Let her try," Igraine said. "There is more to her than meets the eye. I'm sure your teachers thought the same thing when you first trained as a warlock."

Merlin nodded.

"Then it's decided then," De Grance said.

Guinevere bowed her head, her yellow eyes shining.

"Father, princess, king, and prince."

Then she turned and left the room.

16

KATYANA

MERLIN THOUGHT ABOUT GUINEVERE and her magic as the others left the room, and then his thoughts returned to Arthur. He remembered how different he was. He remembered how he refused to return, how he could not see the light. But Merlin knew there was some way to revive him, some way to mend his soul.

"How?" he asked. He knew there were spirits beyond the realm of the living, beyond the realm of Starhearth as well. When the Fallen King Ergar cleansed the Isle of most of the sorcerers, their souls did not ascend to Starhearth, nor were they lost forever. They lingered as part of a parallel dimension, standing by people who could not see them, walking the battlements and roads of this world, yet never truly being here. They watched over the world at night, when fouler things than wolves threatened the light and security of the Isle. But he had never been able to contact them. He wished he could now. He closed his eyes and remembered all the books he had read about the sorcerers and the magic of Demetia. He pictured them before him, and when he opened his eyes, they were stacked upon the table beside his bed. He reached for the one named "The Ancient Sorcerers of Demetia". The book talked about the fall of the ancient kingdom and the cleansing of all witches and warlocks.

But one thing it could not answer was what happened to the warlocks who had sheltered at the Temple of Land's End the day Ergar's armies stormed it. Merlin looked through the books and scriptures for anything regarding communicating with the ancient sorcerers. About Starhearth, there was nothing he didn't know, and about the parallel world, there was almost nothing, only writing that said it was legend. No one, after all, who had gone there, ever returned. Merlin set the books aside and closed his eyes. But rather than aim for Starhearth, he directed his spirit toward the other dimension. He tried to think about the sorcerers of old, thought about the great war that had ultimately fractured the unity that had cost years and thousands of lives to secure. He had never lived through it, but he remembered it. He remembered the fire. He remembered Ergar's crazy blue eyes, his tousled hair, and fearful looks. He remembered the band of anti-sorcerers who emerged from the shadows when he denounced all warlocks. He remembered the ancient magic. By tracing his own line, he found that his own predecessor, King Mergyle, had witnessed the casting of a dragon. The vision he saw was of Demetia City, the capital of Demetia. Four thousand years ago, there was no Land's End, for only King Megolin had established it as a place to be the home of sorcery, for the place from which the guardians of the light cast their spells and controlled the events of time. The dragon that had materialized before Demetia City had been a fire-breathing beast. With scales of steel and amethyst wings, it had soared above the city.

Merlin could see its form racing though the air as it breathed lances of flame. The dragon soared high as the people of Demetia clapped, and then it swooped low. Merlin awoke then and found his spirit lighter. But dread returned when he realized none of that magic made any difference if no one could wield it. Merlin knew he wasn't one of those ancient sorcerers. Merlin knew he wasn't nearly as powerful as the warlocks and witches who had cast dragons and revived the fallen, like his grandfather. Then he remembered Guinevere's energy.

Merlin walked to the door and left the room, his cloak glowing purple. A sudden idea had struck him. And now he needed to see if it was true.

175

With both certain and unsure steps, he found himself walking to the end of the hall, where a guard was standing.

"Where is Lady Guinevere?" he asked.

"She and Lord De Grance and Lord and Lady Megolin have gone to the throne room. Lord De Grance said he does not wish for his court to be disturbed."

"He'll listen to me," Merlin walked away from the guard.

"My lord," he said. "You cannot go to the throne room."

But Merlin wasn't listening anymore. He just walked to the end of this other hall, flew down the stairs to another level, going past guards and servants as he walked.

From outside, starlight was shining through the windows as the torches crackled. And for the first time, Merlin actually saw it as light.

He reached the throne room moments later and stepped through the lord's door. De Grance's councilors were arguing about how best to defend their border with Demetia, and De Grance was listening. Merlin walked straight past his father and a silence fell on the throne room as Merlin stood before his family, Guinevere, and Lord De Grance.

"Merlin," Leo said. "What happened?" Merlin looked at Guinevere. He sensed there was more to her than even she knew. There was a power that she harbored that she did not know how to use, or where it was from.

"I believe your daughter might be the witch who will

revive Arthur." The court did not know what to say. Lady Genie and Lord De Grance stared at him.

"How do you know?"

"A feeling." Merlin looked at Guinevere. And then a vision replaced the world. He was no longer standing amidst the court of Land's End. He was standing by one of the walkways of the Green Keep. The moon was shining bright amidst the stars, and no corner of the sky was left to darkness. Land's End was a maze of torches, with every street lit by iron sconces, and every home by torches and candles. Merlin turned and saw someone standing at the balcony, but their form was ghostly, like the forms of the spirits of Starhearth.

Her eyes glowed yellow, and cloak blue. A guard walked past, not noticing her. And then someone walked toward her. "My lady, you seem disturbed," he said. His cloak glowed blue as well, and his eyes were yellow.

"It's nothing. I just still remember that day," the witch responded.

"We all do, but we can find a way make things right," the wizard said.

"I know. Any premonitions?" The witch asked.

"Not as of yet. For that, I'm grateful."

"Good," the witch looked out beyond the city, and then staggered back.

The warlock turned, his face worried.

"Enya?" he said. But the woman's eyes had gone black. She was seeing a dark vision.

Merlin tried to see what the vision was, but he could not. A minute went by, and then Enya awoke. By this point, other warlocks and witches had joined her.

"What happened? Your eyes turned black," the first warlock said.

Enya looked at him. "Darkness."

"What are you talking about?" Another warlock asked.

Merlin leaned in to hear her talk more clearly. She spoke of the Hun invasion.

"The Huns?" a warlocks said, "but Emperor Constantine is fighting them now. They are weak. They could not possibly be planning to attack the Isle."

"This isn't now. It is some time hence, when the Huns will be commanded by the foulest person who ever walked."

Merlin straightened. So, he was looking at a past from a few decades ago, when the Huns were righting Rome. But he could not recall any woman named Enya from that time. In fact, wasn't Enya one of the great magicians from the years of his ancestor Mergus Megolin?

He leaned forward again, to hear the magicians on the wall better.

"What do you suggest we do?" the first warlock asked Enya. "We cannot change the course of events. We can only direct time."

"So that's what we do. For three thousand years, the Isle has not seen more than a few wizards. De Grance's daughter will be born tonight, but Leo fears that neither she nor his wife will see the dawn. I can hear him. He is praying now. Someone must answer."

The first wizard stroked his beard.

"I will," a younger witch said. Enya turned toward her, yellow eyes glowing.

Merlin, too, turned toward the young witch. Her energy glowed bright and clear, and her face looked kind.

"You know what you will be giving up," Enya said. "Once all good returns, all of us will return to the world as we are, but you will know nothing of yourself."

"Why does this have to happen?" the wizard asked. "Why does Lord De Grance's daughter mean anything?"

"The wizard who returns to the world of the living by her is destined to change the course of the future. What I saw, Toryen, will happen. And a second darkness from which we cannot escape will shroud the Isle if we do not act. De Grance is praying for his daughter to live. It is the only chance we have."

Merlin listened with surprise. They were talking about Guinevere.

"I can do it," the young witch said. "My name is Katyana. I had no family of my own three thousand years ago. I shall have one now. You are my family as well, but I sense we will all perish if this does not happen."

Three thousand years ago. Merlin sucked in a sharp breath. It was a great privilege to look into the Wizard's Plane.

"No," Enya said. "I'll go."

"Enya, you cannot do this," the first wizard said.

"I'm sorry, Toryen. But this has to be done."

Enya smiled at Katyana. "I will not let you give up your life. Twenty years from now, when the fight is here, you will fight from this world, and when the light prevails, you will return to the land of the living."

Katyana shook her head. "I have decided," she said. "I will go. I will not die. And maybe one day, I will remember all of this. Now, I must go."

"Katyana," the one called Toryen said, but she disappeared.

"She cannot be stopped now," Enya said. "We can only hope that her sacrifice will not be for nothing." "We must stop this darkness, or Britannia will never escape from it."

"How?" Toryen asked.

"Lord De Grance prays that his child will survive. His daughter is sick. We will answer his prayer."

Merlin found himself standing near De Grance, but he was not the old, happy man he had met recently. He was far younger. His white hairs were black, and he looked more like sadness personified than greatness.

"Just save her," he prayed.

Katyana walked past Merlin and to De Grance. Then Leo turned and walked back to his child. The midwife was holding her by the fire, trying to wake her. Merlin saw Katyana watching the child, resolving that she might never live as herself again. Then she closed her eyes, she chanted, and she was gone. Then the baby cooed, and Merlin saw as Leo laughed, carrying his child. And then Merlin was standing before the same man, nineteen years later.

Merlin looked at Guinevere, amidst the torches that illuminated the hall, as the members of Lord De Grance's court watched him, and as Megolin and Igraine eyed him. "You are the one who will bring Arthur back. You are more than you think you are. You are more powerful than you think. You are more powerful than even my grandfather."

"What are you talking about?" Guinevere asked.

"You don't know," Merlin said. "I can show you."

Her eyes turned white, and she found herself no longer amidst her family, but standing by the rail of one of the walkways of the keep.

Merlin was there with her.

"Look there," he said. He was looking at a wizard and a witch, standing by the rail.

"How are they sorcerers?"

"Just look."

She looked, and she could hear them talking, but she could not understand what they were talking about. And then Enya said Toryen's name.

"Toryen. He was a sorcerer of the old kingdom."

She listened, and Enya was staggering back. She walked towards them.

At the mention of the Huns, her blood grew cold, and

then colder when she heard Enya say that the Huns would attack decades hence.

"What is this?" She asked Merlin.

"It's your history."

Guinevere could not see it. She listened to the warlocks talking about what she had seen, and then Enya talked about how her father was praying that his daughter live.

"I'll do it," Katyana said.

Guinevere looked at the woman. It was almost like looking at her own reflection. Enya tried to tell the woman that she could not, that what she would be sacrificing, her life, her memories, herself, that she couldn't. Katyana said that she would have a family now, and then she flew up and disappeared, reappearing on the balcony of the chamber where Guinevere had been born. She'd cast dragons here before, and it was where her father told her she would one day be the lady of Land's End, and that she would return the region to its place as the center of sorcery. She saw her father, crying at the rail, praying, right next to where Katyana had appeared. Then her father turned and walked to the midwife who was holding a baby by the fire. Guinevere found herself welling with tears. Her father had told her the story of how he'd nearly lost her, but that a prayer to the heavens had saved her from death. And now she saw Katyana watching the baby. Katyana closed her eyes and began to chant, and Guinevere watched as she disappeared. She heard the baby—herself—cough, and her father laugh, and then she turned to see Merlin.

"I am Katyana."

Merlin nodded. "You are one of the most powerful sorcerers who have ever lived." Merlin said.

Guinevere's parents stared at the two of them with worry etched on their faces.

Guinevere smiled at her father. "The night I was born you said a prayer to the heavens. And the heavens responded. The sorcerers who perished near the end of the War of the Light, they were here that night. They emerge every day at the triple witching hour to watch over the world. And I am Katyana, one of the most powerful sorcerers who ever lived. I knew Enya and Toryen. But I don't remember them. Katyana forgot everything when she became me."

Her father and mother looked at her warily. Perhaps they imagined she was crazy.

"I now know why I have these powers. I've never known what they meant or where they were from. They're Katyana's. That night when I was born, Enya and Toryen were talking about how the Huns would attack Britannia now. They said that I needed to live, that one of them needed to answer your prayer, or else dark things would follow, and the darkness of the Huns would never be defeated. And now I know why. I have to revive Arthur."

Merlin felt relief. For the first time, he trusted that the light would shine, and that the darkness would retreat, but Guinevere did not know how to revive someone. Guinevere had, until now, known nothing more than how to conjure creatures and launch energy. Merlin knew a great deal more, and he did not know how to revive Arthur.

"If this is true," De Grance said, "you must do this. Your mother and I have always known that you were destined for something great. Ever since you were born, you have not been like any other child. But do you know how to revive someone?"

"I can teach her the spells," Merlin said, "but the magic must be hers. And she must be able to heal Arthur. Right now, Arthur does not want to return. And all the magic of the most powerful could not revive him if he does not wish to live again."

"So, how do I stop his suffering?" Guinevere asked.

"I don't know," Merlin said.

"But we'll all figure it out. We have to. Because if Arthur does not return, the world is doomed. Even now, Gallagher is attacking from the north. Cities and towns are being torched. The green fields are turning to desolate wastelands. Gerlach and his foul soldiers are marching toward Gilidor. Demetia is a ruin. And a million more Huns are forming up at ports along the Continental coastline. King Fergus is still allied with them. An army unlike anything the world has ever seen is marching for Land's End.

If we lose this war, the darkness will never be defeated. Whatever chance light finds to shine, it will be snuffed. The North will fall as well, and the Hun banner will fly without opposition.

Winter is near, and if the Huns are not defeated, the cold shall freeze the Isle for all of time."

C.J. BROWN

17

CHANGE OF HEART
ON THE CONTINENTAL COASTLINE

TTILA STOOD ON A KNOLL overlooking the Narrow Sea. Even though the Demetians had been soundly beaten and were on the run, the war was not decisively over. Attila was not conqueror, and the anger he felt of not being the one who drew Arthur's life from his body drove him to new heights.

"I know what I must do," he whispered to all those in his presence, although none of them heard it. They stood there, tired and confused.

Bishkar was still in the north and making his way south without regard to the toll on the size of his forces.

By the time they reached the end, there would hardly be any men left, if Attila guessed aright.

It was time to raise a larger army and put all this to bed.

Stepping back into his tent, he turned to his field commanders and said, "I have had enough of this piecemeal effort. It is time to end this war."

"You want to leave, Sire? You want to return to Germania after we have gotten this far?"

"No, you fool. I want to end this war in our favor. I want to bring more men and end the life of every single peasant on that god-forsaken land."

"You want to raise a new army, Sire?" a faceless general who had recently been promoted to his position asked.

"What is your name?" Attila barked, feeling an unfamiliar presence in his court.

"Din Gar Chuk, sire. I am general of the rear forces. We just got here."

"So, you have yet to see any battle on this land?"

"Yes, Sire."

"Then why do you look as tired as if you have just lost a battle?" Attila asked, disgusted at the man's weakness.

"We just traveled, Sire. We are weary from the journey."

Attila was not impressed. He looked around his tent, a makeshift royal court, in the midst of a command post.

With mud for floors and fresh animal hide as roof, the stench was still palpable in the air.

The faces he wished to see were absent. As much as Biskar annoyed him with his impetuous arrogance, he was like a son to him. Adolphus, now gone, buried along a roadside, tramped by thousands, was the face he truly missed. Adolphus knew how to command men and speak to Attila's heart.

Attila searched the faces around him. In the corner of his tent stood a man different from the rest of the Huns and expendables. He stood, tired, yet polished. His breast plate was not polished, but well maintained. He had seen battle recently, but he was also not one of the Hun forces.

"Who are you?" Attila asked. "You do not look like one of us."

"Indeed, my liege," the stranger answered. "I am not yet one of you, but if you will have me, I would very much like to be. You will find that I can be of great use to you."

"How can you be of use to me?" Attila asked, his voice now tempered by his curiosity.

"First of all, I speak your tongue, as you can witness now, and I also speak the tongue of the Romans. So, the next time you negotiate with them, they will not be able to mock you to your face as you stare ignorantly at their pale faces."

Attila had no response.

The stranger to continued. "I also know the strategy of the enemy. I know where they plan to hide, how they plan to raise more men, and I know how Arthur thinks," the skinny man added.

"You know Arthur, or you know of Arthur?" Attila asked, now more suspicious of the man who had paced up to the front of the tent as he spoke.

"Both. I know him well. I used to stand with him until three nights ago."

"You are from the Isle?" Attila asked, testing his hypothesis of who the stranger might be.

"No. I came to this god-forsaken island not long ago. I left the comfort of my life to follow my general and my king, but now I have had to part ways with him."

"Who is your king and general?"

"You are, my liege," the man answered.

"Not at this minute, but before you came to me."

"Lucius was my emperor, and Arthur, my general. I was there when he killed Adolphus."

At the sound of this, Attila rushed to the stranger and stood within a breath of him.

"You are Arthur Pendragon's aide, are you not? The man who has been riding next to that creature since his first day as a soldier."

"Yes, my name is Vipsanius, my liege."

"Spy. Arrest this man," Attila shouted.

The guards that stood beyond the walls of skin enduring the cold air and the soft mud rushed into the tent and surrounded the stranger.

"You can arrest me, torture me, or kill me. I will

accept one or all three options. But one way or another I had to try. I can no longer spend another day on the losing side of this equation. I could have joined the ranks of the Romans who have joined you and fought with them if I were a spy. I could have lied about my true identity and blended in, if I were a spy. Instead, I chose to speak truth and join your cause."

Attila eyed him, looking for any hint of deception. The man looked tired, but well trained. Unlike the rest of the Huns who were already tired from the journey, this man seemed to be able to hold his composure even if he was from the losing side.

"Why should I take in a loser?" Atilla asked.

"Because if I were on your side, I would be a winner. Take me, use me, allow me to make a living. If you find me unworthy, kill me at any time, even if it is just for amusement or sport."

Attila liked that idea, and there was one way he could maximize this good fortune. "Ride with me and tell me all you know of Arthur and his plans."

"Yes, my liege. Where are we going?"

"To raise the largest army the world has ever seen."

NEWSLETTER

This is the fifth book in the Pendragon Legend. To get earliest news of the sixth installment in this series, make sure to sign up for C.J. Brown's newsletter using the link below.

NEWSLETTER SIGNUP FORM

ABOUT THE AUTHOR

C.J. Brown has a lifelong passion for fantasy books, and she quit her career in marketing to pursue her dream of becoming an author. Legends and myths in particular strike her fancy, and she loves putting her own spin on them. An adventurer at heart, when not writing, she can be found exploring the old mystical Northwoods around her home, where she finds much of her inspiration.

Website: cj-brown.com
Facebook: fb.me/cjbrown78

Thanks for reading. Please consider leaving a review—it means a lot!

ALSO BY C.J. BROWN

Printed in Great Britain
by Amazon

23644279R20112